Dregs

By Barri L. Bumgarner

Tigress Press, LLC

Copyright © 2007, Barri L. Bumgarner
Cover design and layout © 2007, Just Ink
Print Book Format:
ISBN-10: 0-9793857-0-9
ISBN-13: 978-0-9793857-0-4

First Printing April, 2007

Published in the United States of America
Tigress Press, LLC
Columbia, MO 65202
www.tigresspress.com

Acknowledgements

So many people helped with this project along the way.

The usual suspects: my novels group (Brian, Elaine, Heidi, Margo); Marsha, as always, for reading it a bajillion times; my new publicist, Chloie Piveral, for all her hard work in getting this book on the map; Jill Womack at TRYPS, for opening my eyes to making *Dregs* a staged reading and the importance of this becoming a play; Dana Harris, for the statistics and documentation into recognizing bullies, teasing, and all that leads to school violence (and for reading it, too!); Jan Summers and Helen Cope for early read-throughs, and Jan for doing it again! A big thanks to Terry Trueman and Todd Strasser for taking time out of your busy schedules to read this novel...both of you inspired me! Elaine Lanmon, a huge thank you for an amazing cover! Tam Adams, for somehow making me look more photogenic than I am. And to Janet Musick for always making my work more polished and ready to go.

There are so many other people who've suffered to raise awareness for school shootings.

I began *Dregs* in March of 1998, still a year before the tragedy that made Columbine High School synonymous with school violence. Within five months, there would be fatal shootings at Pearl, Mississippi; Jonesboro, Arkansas; and Paducah, Kentucky. This rash of violence horrified and enlightened me. For all the victims, not only those who lost their lives but also those who suffered the daily put-downs that left no perceived out other than violence, this story is for you. The vicious cycle of clique superiority can only be broken if adults expect the same behavior from all kids, even those who excel in sports.

Hopefully, *Dregs* will help make teachers, parents, and students aware that cliques in schools have lasting effects. For information, go to www.dontteasehotline.org

To anyone out there who thinks this could happen to you or this could be you, please get help. Visit: http://youthviolence.edschool.virginia.edu/bullying/bullying-links.html

Parents, more information exists to help identify the problem and/or recognize the signs: www.myoutofcontrolteen.com

Dedication

For all the victims, the survivors, and the families. The more awareness raised, the less likely it is that kids have died in vain.

And for Sammie...

Benson's Journal

Monday, September 15th

    If I could rank my life on a scale of 1-10, I'd have to resort to negative numbers. Mrs. Mattingly, this journal writing for your class isn't such a bad thing, because today SUCKED.

    That freshman jerk-off Steve Ralston shoved Ryan into a locker, proving his manhood to everybody at Westwood by pushing around a seventh grader. Oooh. It's proof that jocks are stupid. We were late to P.E. because of it, and Coach Rohart just laughed when I tried to explain. Yes, if you're wondering, Coach would fall under that previous "jock" comment, too. Except...why is he so fat? I mean, a PE teacher should be like, in shape... shouldn't he? Colin said he used to be, that Coach was a lineman or something, and that the bulking up catches up with you...reasons two through ten not to be a jock, right?

    Sorry, I know I shouldn't diss a teacher, but does he really count? After he quit laughing, he gave us a tardy, then proceeded to tell the entire class that I didn't seem to take after my older brother. Most of the seventh graders didn't think it was funny – they've known me long enough to understand my dilemma – but the few freshmen retards almost hurt themselves laughing. Wanted to tell them they were losers for having to take general P.E. What moron can't get into freshman athletics or weightlifting?

Considering having Coach Rohart assassinated, but I'm not sure I have enough in my piggy bank. Could swipe some from Colin's hidden stash – that would be fitting. I can see the headline now: Sixteen-year-old star funds coach's assassination. I think I like it. Going to hunt for cash now.

Chapter 1

BENSON SCHMIDT HATED his older brother more than lima beans rolled in spinach and sprinkled with cow manure. Even without the manure, he'd hate Colin.

"Ah, poor Bennie, you're such a *girl*. When I was in seventh grade, I..." Colin cocked his head, grinning. The blond hair, dimples, and bright blue eyes lured the girls, but to Benson, it meant nothing but trouble. And being his mirror image just made it worse.

"Yeah, yeah, I know, you were stud quarterback, hotshot point guard, and Mr. All-America. And I'm not. God, I'm so SICK of hearing that crap!" Benson fought the tears, lying on the floor with Colin straddling him, a serious case of Indian torture pending.

It's the way every afternoon worked after Colin's football practice during the hour before their mom got home from the firm. The season determined Colin's aggression – the sophomore phenom tackled and tortured during football, bounced Benson off furniture picks throughout basketball, and hurled hostile projectiles during baseball.

"Truth hurts, weenie-breath." Colin rolled up his sleeves and flexed his bulging biceps, giving Benson just the opportunity he needed to squirm out from under his brother.

Even if Colin was three years older, Benson wasn't the geek he pretended to be at school. Maybe it made him a poser, but he'd rather hang out in the shadows than be compared to Colin in the spotlight.

He ducked the pillow before it pummeled him, and raced up the stairs to his bedroom. He slammed and locked the door, panting as he leaned against it.

"I hope you throw twenty interceptions Friday night!" Benson screamed, then wished he hadn't. Egging Colin on was the worst thing to do, even if Mom should be home any time. He held his breath for a solid thirty seconds before realizing Colin wasn't coming to beat him senseless.

I hate you! Benson wanted to scream, but why bother?

Without a weapon, he was no match for his brother. Colin outweighed him, out-muscled him, out-everythinged him. Benson could never measure up, so he had stopped trying. Other than soccer, he had no unique skills of his own. It all tied back to something his mother, father, or brother did first – and better. So he ditched sports on principle. Even soccer.

His best friend Ryan possessed a more callous disregard for put-downs and had lots more practice at it, given his runt stature. And so could Benson, at school. But Colin brought out the evil in him.

His chest hurt from the Indian torture, and he was so frustrated he wanted to cry. There wouldn't be any point in tattling. It had never helped in the past. Besides, how would he fit that into dinner conversation?

Yep, scouts're gonna be watchin' Colin go for the single season rushing record Friday night and, by the way, he beat me up again today.

Yeah, right.

He dropped onto his bed, resigned to his menial existence as Colin's shadow. Grabbing the phone, he hit speed dial one. Ryan would have insight, would give him a boost, and perhaps have ideas on how he could off Colin once and for all.

Murder wasn't out of the question, was it?

"What's up, Bennie? I got loads of homework... Sorry. I'm down to a 95% in Algebra." Ryan sighed.

"Oooooh, gonna blow that straight A honor roll. What's up with that?" Benson let out a half-hearted laugh. "I swear, Ryan, when I get his size, I'm gonna plow him every chance I get."

Benson sat up so he could see his reflection in the mirror, flexing and inspecting his small ball of bicep.

"By the time you're his size, Ben, he'll be playin' for the Packers." Ryan snickered, then started babbling about the math assignment. Benson couldn't deal with homework now. He was still pissed. His stud brother had the whole school, town, and especially their parents, completely snowed. They would eat dog poop out of the palm of his hand if he told them it was chocolate pudding. That riled Benson more than the daily taunts and beatings.

"I'll vent about him in my journal. You get yours done yet?"

"Yeah, but I'm gonna run out of the things to say pretty quick. I'm not the writer you are. More money in math and science."

"Geek," Benson challenged.

"Loser," Ryan countered. It was a game that could go on for several minutes until the slurs got too vulgar or one of them ran out.

"Well, I gotta go. Mom's cookin' dinner, and I'm thinking I might help her." Benson sat up and stared at his reflection in the mirror. He finger-combed his hair while studying a new crop of zits. He'd tackle those after dinner.

"Must be cooking something good, huh?"

"Fried chicken."

"Ah, and you're going to set the table while you eat a drumstick before Colin gets them all." Ryan chuckled, and it amazed Benson how well his best friend knew him.

"Exactly. See you tomorrow, and don't forget to bring your science homework. I might need to look at it." Benson intended to give it an attempt, but why bother when Ryan's was as good as an answer key?

"No problem, man, but you owe me. As always."

Who had time for science when he had murders to plot?

Ryan's Journal

Monday, Sept. 15th

    I'm considering a serious assignment for our Publications project - nothing fluffy or too geeky. With topics due by Thursday, I was thinking about Benson and all the crap he goes through with Colin, and my problems with Ralston. Why do popular kids think they're all that? I mean, who made these rules, and why do all the rest of us tolerate it? There are way more of us than them.

    Anyway, we could shake up the junior high social structure and call it Operation Cappuccino - I'm tired of being the dregs in the coffee cup of cliques. (Nice, huh?) And we could interview all the popular kids, give them a taste of what it feels like to be us.

    I have some pretty cool ideas. I'll run it by Benson tomorrow. I told him I had already journaled my first entry, so I couldn't bring it up on the phone. Secret's between you and me, Mrs. Matt. You said these were confidential, and I'm trusting you. I tell Benson everything. Except on the rare occasion when I lie to him.

If this is like a confessional, is it okay to admit to you that I dream regularly of Steve Ralston getting depantsed in front of the entire school?

Operation Cappuccino Outline
Publications Plan Due Monday

<u>Thesis statement for article</u>: Who determines what makes a teenager popular and who made these rules? How fragile is popularity? Can we mix it up so the top isn't so far from the bottom?

<u>Goal of article</u>: Reveal how cliques make the unpopular feel. Show how things the privileged do every day – exclusive tables at lunch, putting someone down for how they dress, always being the center of attention for everything – makes the rest of us feel. Also try to expose the backstabbing that goes on at ALL levels.

<u>Groups to Interview</u>: Preps, jocks, skaters, goths, a few dregs, losers and wannabes. Oh, and don't forget the cheerleaders.

<u>Specific people to interview</u>: Michael Barker, Malakai Jeffries, Evan Anderson, Steve Ralston, Nikki Harmon, Allison _____, Lisa _____, and Jenni something or other and maybe one other cheerleader (don't know their last names – we'll call them all Barbie for now), Calli Matthews and his girlfriend (she's a great female jock!). Also interview Tim Silvey and Pam Utterbeck.

<u>Questions for preps, jocks, & cheerleaders:</u> Who're your real friends? What makes that person a friend? Who would stick by your side if you lost status? What if you lost the ability to perform (whatever it is that specific person is good at that adds to or makes them popular)? Why do you think you're popular and other kids aren't? What would happen to your popularity if your dad got busted for drug possession? What do you think makes someone popular? (Try to let them see that the friend might be more superficial than they think...the idea is to reveal weaknesses). Also want to narrow the gap between them and us.

<u>Notes</u>: Make sure to take good notes and audiotape if possible. Take every opportunity to disprove the stereotypes – that's the point, isn't it? Not just theirs, but ours, too.

<u>Key Element</u>: They care what other people think – play on that!

Chapter 2

STEVE RALSTON SMACKED Ryan's books out of his hands, then backed him against the lockers. "You get it?"

Benson looked frantically up and down the hall, then around the corner toward Publications class. They were going to be late. Was that Ralston's plan?

"No... What do you mean by a free day? Free from what?" Ryan's face was beet red, but Benson couldn't think of anything to do to help.

"A free day from me, runt. You cough up twenty bucks, and I'll leave your ass alone. Whaddya say?" Ralston, freshman linebacker, star forward, and all-city shot putter, towered more than a head taller than Ryan. He shoved Ryan against the bank of lockers and lifted the seventh grader's feet at least six inches off the ground. Ralston loomed close enough that Benson thought the thug might bite his best friend's nose off.

Or kiss him. God, I bet if I said that, Ralston would leave Ryan alone. Kill me, maybe.

"Wanna run me a tab?" Ryan quipped. Benson froze, his hand on his wallet, ready to spot his buddy the bill if he needed it.

He's gonna plow your face, Ryan. Are you off your rocker?

Ten or fifteen other seventh, eighth, and ninth graders held their breath. Two or three girls giggled at Ryan's response. No one moved when Ralston lowered Ryan and snarled at him. Steve slammed his fist into the locker inches from Ryan's head with a startling *whack*. The second hour tardy bell rang, and Mrs. Mattingly came barreling around the corner, late for her own class.

"What's going on here, boys?" She opened her classroom door, head-nodded for everyone to either get in her room or get on to their own. For an older teacher, well into her forties, Benson assumed, she was pretty in a fun sort of way and had bright green eyes. It was hard not to notice her. She smiled all the time. Most of the boys couldn't help but stare, and the girls wanted to be just like her.

The hall cleared quickly, but Benson hadn't missed the stiff set of Ryan's jaw – admired it even.

"Yeah, he bit off more than he could chew this time." Ryan pointed at the dispersing crowd and the spot where Ralston had disappeared around the corner, then strutted into class. Everyone giggled again, knowing Steve couldn't hear or otherwise their short friend would've had a mouthful of blood and broken teeth.

Once they took their seats at the various round tables throughout the room – one of the things the kids liked best about Publications class – Ryan laid out his plan for Benson.

"What's a dreg?" Benson asked.

"The dregs, you know, the crud left at the bottom of a coffee cup. That's us. You know, those of us at the bottom. Christ, Bennie, don't play dumb." Ryan let out a long sigh and ran a hand through unruly red hair, rolling his hazel eyes.

"I ain't a dreg. I'm just not Colin."

"You *choose* not to be like Colin though. You're tall enough, smart enough, and a good enough athlete. You fall into this category by default, Bennie."

"Shut-up, four eyes," Benson barked, acting madder than he really was. Ryan knew not to take the bites seriously. Otherwise, they would never speak to each other.

His best friend witnessed almost daily the crap Benson went through at home. Being the younger brother of the town's prodigy took its toll, and even though Ryan was an only child, he hung around the Schmidt household enough to understand hardcore sibling rivalry.

"So maybe you got something here. If they're the big dogs and we're the dregs, how do we take this and make it work? God knows we got firsthand experience." Benson leafed through his papers and reviewed the assignment. Mrs. Mattingly had detailed the objectives and all the requirements, and since it wasn't even mid-term, they had nearly four weeks to complete it.

"This is gonna be good, Bennie, and maybe make my life a little easier along the way. No more dregs in the coffee cup of life for us, man. We'll let Operation Cappuccino speak for us from now on."

"Operation Cappuccino – that's cool. I don't know what the heck it means, but it sounds awesome." Benson sat back while Ryan motioned to Mrs. Matt. He wasn't holding his breath for life-altering changes. He just wanted a little peace.

After a ten-minute explanation and both barely tethering their enthusiasm, Mrs. Matt finally said, "You have an outstanding idea here, boys. *But*..." She held their proposal in one hand, her reading glasses in the other. She squinted, tiny lines around her sparkling eyes splaying out like spokes. As usual, she set down her glasses and twirled a lock of streaked blonde hair around a finger. Benson didn't understand how she could be ten years older than his mom but act so much younger. She possessed none of the *I'm an adult and you're not* attitude.

"But?" Benson set his copy of their plan on the table. Mrs. Matt had to approve the concept before they could launch it and, until now, it hadn't occurred to Benson that she might not.

"*But*...remember we're here to offer a fresh perspective. You're striving for the George Polk Award for journalism, not a headline in the *National Inquirer*. In other words, I know what's *not* written here. Operation Cappuccino is clever yet simple and, I have to admit, the most creative one submitted. Even the name is catchy."

Benson couldn't conceal his excitement.

Mrs. Matt put up her hand to stop him. "Don't get ahead of yourself, Benson. Steve Ralston got three days of after-school detention for slamming Ryan into a locker two weeks ago. Remember, Ryan? Steve didn't get to play the whole first half against Parkway South because of it, so I'm sure he's pretty upset. He probably won't break Westwood's single season sack record now." She cocked an eyebrow, giving them time to consider her warning.

And Colin's thrilled about that – he's only held that record for a year. But Benson knew better than to tell Mrs. Matt that. It was important to disguise his hatred of everything Colin-like.

"And, Benson, you had to get an administrator to get Ryan out of a P.E. closet a week or so before that, right? This better not be a vendetta, boys." Mrs. Matt paused, looking from Benson to Ryan and back. "This idea to interview students from different cliques to determine what causes popularity *or not* is sticky. You come from a unique background in that regard, Benson. Are you willing to use personal experiences?" She continued, no longer twisting hair but chewing on the arm's end of her reading glasses.

Benson fought the heat rising in his neck and ears, suppressing the familiar anger welling in his chest. *Chill, Benson, chill.* "Uh, yes, ma'am. I, um, me and Colin may see things from a different view, but we're approaching this as journalists. We can be objective." He studied his copy of the proposal so he wouldn't have to meet his favorite teacher's steady gaze. It wasn't just Mrs. Matt's bright green eyes or long wavy blonde hair that made it hard to look away. She was the kind of teacher no one wanted to disappoint. Even if she had hit below the belt, he guessed what she said was just observation.

We're not going to lie...we just wanna give people a dose of reality.

"I don't doubt that, Benson. But I see that gleam in your eye. In the first four weeks of this class, you've been pretty talkative. You make good grades, most of the kids like you, and you're handsome. Quite frankly, you're a walking contradiction. You're not a *dreg*... You're stereotyping yourself by saying you are." She furrowed her brow for a minute, sending Benson's heart into his throat. *She's gonna say no.* "What's your real purpose here? I mean I need to see a clear-cut goal." Mrs. Matt set the papers down and stared at Benson, obviously expecting an explanation.

"We want to bridge the gap. It isn't about bringing them down, but I guess it's more to show them we're not all that different." Benson ran an unsteady hand across his closely cropped sandy blond hair. "I think the idea is that the cappuccino machine will mix us up better." He looked over at Ryan. "Right?"

"Exactly," Ryan agreed.

"You boys have a big idea and your premise is good, but be careful not to be guilty of what you're judging other people of doing...does that make sense?" Mrs. Matt didn't wait for an answer. "I want daily updates on this, and I want to approve all interview questions before you ask them. Understood?" She picked up the proposal, marked her initials in the box at the bottom, and slid it across the table to the two of them.

"Absolutely. You won't be disappointed, I guarantee it!" Benson snatched the page and beamed. Ryan jabbed an elbow in his ribs, doing everything possible to suppress a smile.

Our gold ticket to Hollywood, he wanted to blurt, but he'd never admit he watched *Idol* with his mom. Not in a million years.

"I want to know who you're interviewing and when. I want to know why you're choosing each person you talk to. This is going to be done *carefully,* boys." Mrs. Mattingly stood and motioned for them to get back to their seats and start on their interview questions.

They scampered to a back corner table and started making a list...potential questions, perfect targets, and the best order to do it in. They barely heard the bell when it rang, both running to third hour, and for the first time since seventh grade started, Benson had something to look forward to.

I might be a dreg, but at least I don't have as far to fall.

Operation Cappuccino Feedback Sheet

Comments from Mrs. Matt: I have two issues with your project... First of all, I don't want this to turn into popularity bashing. I trust both of you, but I want to make sure you stay objective. So I need the following things from you...your goal, your intended outcome, and why you've chosen this as your project. Also, a little explanation of the title might enlighten me a bit as well. Other than that, this is an amazing endeavor, and I'm really proud of both of you...just remember that dating the captain of the football team, or being one, doesn't make you cuter or more likely to succeed. Michael Jordan wasn't even a starter in high school...think about that, okay?

Goal: (Benson's answer) *At first I think we intended to show the popular kids they weren't superior. But the more we researched and talked, our goal changed. We want to make everyone at the top of the social ladder realize their life isn't so much better than ours. My mom said junior high and high school were some of the hardest years of her life, and she was the student body president and a homecoming queen! So I want everybody to see that we're all equal, even if we're on different rungs of that ladder. Height is relative to perspective and aspirations.*

Intended Outcome: (Ryan's answer) *Like Benson said, we really want to decrease the divide between the preps and the dregs. We don't necessarily want to knock them down, just lower them a bit and move us up. Does that make sense? And we don't plan to be underhanded, Mrs. Matt, I swear. We just need to ask questions to show them that being popular doesn't make them better. I think Benson's got a unique insight. Colin is Mr. All-America in everything he does, but we've decided* *it's hard to tell if that's a good thing – he doesn't always seem so thrilled by it. We just want, in some small way, to bridge the gap between all the cliques. Everybody focuses on the achievement gap, well, we're more worried about the clique gap.*

Why this project: (Benson's answer with lots of Ryan's input) *When Ryan told me it was called Operation Cappuccino, I didn't get it at first. But then when he explained to me what a dreg was, you know, that stuff at the bottom of the coffee cup, being the machine that mixes us all back together sounded really cool. Like that kid in Pay It Forward. We could be part of something really big, you know, something that really makes a difference. We want to show kids from all cliques that they can be high-priced latte if they want it. It's not limited to the most popular. We may not all shop at the same stores and wear the same clothes – or drink the same coffee – but we could if we wanted, right? That's why... we want the Tim Silveys of the world to realize he could be Steve Ralston if he really wanted to be. And vice versa. Maybe some of the popular kids would like a day or two out of the spotlight.*

Benson's Journal

Tuesday, Sept. 16th

    Today, for the 1st time, I went to lunch as an investigator, not a loser. Wow, are they conformists! I never noticed it before. The front 3 tables where all of "them" eat are like magnets for the wannabes. The jocks at one table, cheerleaders at another, and the gang-banger athletes at the 3rd. Then they flock around each other like maggots on crap. (Sorry, Mrs. Matt, I'll be nicer about things, but it's true!)

    Watched for a while, and decided even if I'm a nobody, at least I don't disappoint anybody but myself. Coming in to the Westwood Cafeteria with Operation Cappuccino on my mind sure gave me a different attitude. I didn't even care if they threw stuff at me or called me names. Which, btw, they didn't. Weird, huh?

    Kids roamed around those tables like mindless sheep. The rank of popularity starts from there – the pretty people flaunting their status, and the kids in back envying it.

    Well, not all of them…That's what's so cool. My friends all like each other because we've always liked each other. Not because of what we do, how much we have, and how we dress. It must be hard work pleasing everybody else all the time.

Chapter 3

THE NEXT DAY at lunch, Benson analyzed the cafeteria with a reporter's eye.

The first table changed with the sports season – uniforms and enough blue and gold to wallpaper the gym. Most of the other two hundred Westwood Jays surrounding them aspired to occupy a seat there. *I'm sure Colin had a reserved spot at the jock and the rah-rah table.*

Closest to the food checkout lines, football jerseyed boys or athletic clones in Hilfiger, Polo, or Fubu sat laughing and stuffing food in their mouths. Evan Anderson, Michael Barker, and Steve Ralston, freshman gods, delighted in the swooning attention from the mass of worshippers.

Benson studied them, like a scientist peering into a microscope, and felt an odd pity for them. For their conformity, their inability to stand alone, their need for the spotlight.

The second table toward the center teemed with ponytails and bouncing blue-and-gold skirts. One thing Benson understood already was that the saying on the lockers was true.

Athlete by nature, cheerleader by choice. Except that the choice usually didn't belong to the individual but to the overall concept of what a cheerleader should look like, act like, and how she giggled. Those were mighty prerequisites.

Nikki Harmon and some fake blonde burst into a fit of fake laughter, as if on cue.

"Shut up, Nikki. I did *not!*"

"Did, too."

"Did not."

"Oh, get over yourself, girl. You know you did."

Like I'm so sure, like for real, like you're a total idiot. Benson rolled his eyes, though he was sure none of them would notice.

The third table's uniform was less mainstream. Puffy sports coats, NFL jerseys, and bandana-wrapped calves signified which side the group represented. Bloods and Crips were not a myth in Jamestown or in junior high, even if just for show or intimidation. The school had policies against gang-banging, but the kids always managed to show their loyalty.

Once the necessity of eating was out of the way, the three tables mingled – the elite gabbing, flirting – superiority evident in every movement they made. They dominated the view because swarms of eighth and ninth graders swirled around them like fat kids to French fries.

Benson eyed them, assessing who to interview first. *The elite, my ass. They're followers, every single one of 'em.*

He could honestly say that, in seven years of school, he probably hadn't spoken to any of them in two or three years, not on purpose anyway. Red Rover on the playground in fourth grade had been the last straw. Why did sixth graders put so much effort into picking on little kids, anyway?

A bobbing head in the back of the crowded lunchroom jerked him off the dirty Field Elementary playground. A voice could be heard faintly over the din. Benson could picture Ryan – glasses slipping down his pug nose, Palm Pilot bouncing in his front pocket.

"Bennie! Back here!"

He locked in on Ryan's yo-yoing head and weaseled around classmates.

It was only the fourth week of school, and everyone had settled in their fixed places, more obedient of it than a teacher's seating chart. No one had consulted any of the twenty or thirty kids in the back rows but, for most of them, out of sight suited them just fine.

"You get your science done in Study Hall?" Ryan asked, scooting his lunch bag out of Benson's way. The center of this particular table had a giant peace sticker in the middle of it, much like the ones on every notebook or binder Ryan Laughlin carried. Peace advocate was a tag he wore proudly and loudly, he had declared at the beginning of the year, boycotting both the war and bullies. Benson figured Ryan was more likely to impact Iraq than the upperclassmen who had picked on him since stepping foot on his first school bus.

Wishful thinking...

"Yep, and I've written some notes for our project. Wanna work on it after school?" A few of their other friends started jabbering, asking what their topic was. But neither divulged anything, for fear of either jinxing it or having someone steal their idea.

"Ah, c'mon, Bennie. There are games today. And they start right after school. It's research for the project. What do you say?" Ryan, oblivious of his social standing, wanted to be involved – never as a participant but happy to be in the hub of the cheering section. Regardless of how it could turn on him.

"Which side we rootin' for?" Benson cocked an eyebrow, trying to rile him.

"C'mon, Schmitty, it's our first year of junior high, and with Operation Cappuccino, things are gonna be different. We don't have to be dregs – we can be high price *latte.*" Ryan nodded his head too emphatically, making Benson grin. He just couldn't ward off the contagious goofy bug Ryan always seemed infected with.

"Operation Cappuccino?" a tablemate asked. "What the heck is that?"

"Bringing expensive coffee to Westwood," Ryan dead-panned. "Sick of milk."

Benson bit his lip. *Good one.* "You're gonna wake up one day and say, 'Dang, I was such a dork in junior high. What the heck was up with that?'" Benson smacked his buddy hard on the back, almost knocking Ryan into his PBJ.

"Nope, I don't think so. Besides, look at all the new kids! When we start our project, it'll be a whole new pot of coffee." Ryan beamed.

Benson belched laughter as he took a gulp of Powerade, then went into a coughing fit. When he could breathe again, he inspected the tables around them and realized Ryan was right.

In the first few weeks of school, he'd been too worried about himself to notice everyone else. The back row was filled with dregs, geeks, and misfits. Goth kids wandered from table to table trying not to conform, but conforming in their effort to do so. Nondescript kids in hand-me-downs – ripped, faded, out of style – chatted with others seething with mediocrity. Scores of kids Benson had never seen before. Ciphers hid their eyes from the world and sat in isolated silence. A few typical brainiacs did homework while they ate.

Benson gave his classic crooked grin, never good at resisting his best friend's excitement. "Operation Cappuccino better live up to snuff."

Ryan looked toward the front of the lunchroom. "Oh, it will, Bennie. It will."

"Steve's up there being worshipped. Should I kick it off with him?" Benson raised his eyebrows.

"Oooh, he's perfect. You got study hall with him third hour, too. Start with him tomorrow. Then we'll have the weekend to let him simmer down." Ryan lifted his own eyebrows, and added, "So how 'bout the game?"

"God, you're such a poser." Benson shook his head, amazed and a little anxious. "I guess. But I'm ain't staying for Ralston's game."

"*Sweet!*" Ryan play-jabbed Benson's jaw, then flipped open a spiral notebook. "We're gonna change Westwood, Bennie, mark my words."

"By going to a game?" No matter how much he admired Ryan, he wished his best friend didn't dream of righting every wrong. But then again, Ryan marched to the beat of his own maracas. "I don't have to cheer, do I?"

"Jesus, Schmitty, you're a loser, ya know that?" Ryan shook his head.

"Huh-uh, I know what you're really thinkin'. You're wonderin' how I can be so totally boss and it not rub off on you, right?" Benson chuckled, always happy to spread a heavy dose of sarcasm.

"Yep, that's it, Bennie. I got weenie envy. But I'm thinking I prefer my brains over – over... What is it you got that I'd want again?" Ryan slapped the table in exaggerated fits of laughter, then added with a completely straight face, "Besides, no one says *boss* anymore."

"Hey, guys, watch this!" A geek with thick glasses and mismatched clothes motioned from the table beside them.

A boy with shocking red hair, a friend they had called Scooter since first grade, took a huge swig of milk. He stared at his audience, his face turning as red as his hair, then sent milk spraying from his nose.

"Oh, man!" one kid moaned.

"Yuck!"

"Dude, that's so gross!"

Benson and Ryan were rolling. Benson nearly snorted his own drink as he clutched his side and tried to breathe.

"Do it again, Scooter, do it again!" someone shouted.

"No, man, don't. I'll never be able to drink milk again! No wonder you guys're such losers." Tim Silvey, fellow dreg with anger management issues, threw his half-empty carton into a nearby trashcan. "At least pretend you got some class."

Don't be a spoil sport, Benson started, but caught himself. Tim stalked away, and it occurred to Benson that it was going to be an uphill battle if they were going to change the social structure. But Ryan was right. Why not?

No one said they had to be dregs forever.

Ryan's Journal

Wednesday, September 17th

 Ball game today kicked butt. That goon Larry Wyatt (Wyatthead by those of us who know and tolerate him) stuffed his snow cone down the back of my shirt during the game, said it was an accident, but I know the truth. We were cheering, and I said something like, "Man, I can't believe those guys are the same age as me!" He chirped (he sounds like a bird, Mrs. Matt, for real), "Ain't nothing about them and you the same, Laughlin," then ACCIDENTALLY dropped his rainbow snow cone down the back of my shirt. I pretended I didn't really care, and that burst his bubble pretty quick. He likes big reactions, probably because he's trying to exercise his pea-sized brain (sorry, Mrs. Matt – it is okay to vent in my journal, isn't it? It offers great incentive).

 Anyway, we won both the 7th and 8th grade games. I was gonna stay for the last one, but Colin showed up and got under Benson's skin. I don't know why he lets it bother him so much. Then again, I don't know why Colin likes to come be worshipped by jr. high kids either. He's a freakin' sophomore. But I guess that's what you do when you get your license. You try to go to a bunch of places where people will notice that you HAVE your license. And Colin saved all that money and bought a sweet used RX-7 – awesome sound system and dual mufflers specially installed. Benson calls it the Crap Mobile, but I know he'd love it if it were his.

I can't imagine what it would feel like to have my brother be so insanely popular that everyone in school wants to be just like him. Or at least have his attention. I hope Benson doesn't let Colin distort his views, being the hub of the Jock Straps and the Barbie Brigade. Benson gets so ticked off at everything "Colin."

I guess it's my job to run interference. Friends gotta be able to count on each other, especially with a brother who's gonna be famous.

Chapter 4

SITTING AT HIS assigned table in study hall, Benson rehearsed the introduction.

Hi, Nikki. You haven't spoken to me in two or three years except to call me a dork, but I'd really like to interview you for Publications...

"Crap," he muttered, second-guessing their project. Talking about it and actually *doing* it were two totally different things.

Dating the captain of the football team, or being one, doesn't make you cuter or more likely to succeed, Mrs. Matt had said. But had Mrs. Matt ever gotten a swirly?

I bet she was popular... In fact, he'd stake his life on it.

Nothing humiliated a person more than having his head shoved in a flushing toilet. *Why the heck did we think a few stupid questions would change all that?*

Benson took several minutes to muster the courage to approach the rah-rah table. After the stupid football game last night, he had gone home and hidden in his bedroom, door locked to punctuate his insecurity. He didn't come down for dinner, didn't bother with his homework – not even his journaling – and decided the encounter with Colin was the first of many he would have to endure. They would never be in the same school together – *thank God* – but Jamestown was too small, and Colin was too big for him to avoid for the next three years.

Just thinking about it spurred Benson into action. If ever he needed motivation to topple the system, Colin provided it.

He took a deep breath and crossed the cafeteria, never looking up to see who was watching. He stopped at the study hall teacher's table and explained about his project, how he needed to interview some students. Mrs. Yarbrough raised her

eyebrows, clearly surprised, but then smiled and told him to
keep it as quiet as he could.

With the green light, he realized there was no turning back.
Not brave enough for jocks yet, he started as close to the top as
he had the nerve for. He dove in headfirst before she could
look up and tell him to beat feet.

"Hey, Nikki, can I talk to you a minute?" His voice
trembled a little. *I could make it to the door and she might
never realize I ever said anything...*

But she didn't seem quite so intimidating sitting by herself.
The one-student-per-table rule would make the assignment
ten times easier. The popular got their strength from the pack,
he and Ryan had decided. *Sort of like killer bees.*

Nikki Harmon, one of Westwood's elite eighth grade cheerleaders, glanced up at him, snarled her lip, and returned to her
math book. She tucked a loose strand of dark hair behind her
ear, the rest restrained in a low ponytail, aside from a few
bangs dangling in her eyes.

"I gotta finish my Algebra." She flitted her ponytail about
like she was flipping him off.

"It's for the school paper, the Westwood Examiner. Your
name will be in the article and... and if you don't want to be
featured, I'll find someone else. I understand. Thanks anyway."
The words came out too fast as Benson backed away slowly,
giving the well-tanned girl a chance to change her mind. Her
dark hair and features made her look like an actress he had
seen in a movie once – some chick who thought she was
Indiana Jones – except Nikki wasn't nearly as pretty. Her
features weren't quite symmetrical, something that would've
gotten her teased if she didn't wear a Westwood skirt, live in a
rich neighborhood, and date Mr. All-America. Which one
didn't matter.

The flaw hadn't gotten past Benson while he was writing
his questions.

"You work for the paper? What's your name?" Nikki
dropped her pen, suddenly all ears.

Her tone wasn't exactly friendly, but it had taken a turn
from snotty to lukewarm. He had started with Nikki so he

could hone his skills before approaching the real target – *Steve Ralston.*

"Benson Schmidt, and yes, I work for the paper." His heart raced as he concentrated to keep his hands still.

"Well, Benson Schmidt, have a seat. Are you a seventh grader?" Her long eyelashes fluttered over her chocolate eyes, making it hard for him to focus. Maybe not a beauty queen, but Nikki Harmon had that *it* factor. She stared at him, judging him, sizing him up. He was doing the same. Her right eye was significantly bigger than her left, and a tad higher.

"Yep, I'm the new meat." Benson grinned, trying to set Nikki at ease. If he acted scared, she would be too superior. It was important she see him as an equal, if that were possible.

We're gonna be high priced coffee from now on. Can't you just taste it?

Ryan had belted Benson for not answering, but now Benson had a strong opinion on the matter. Why did popularity determine so much when it was never a choice in the first place?

"Okay," Benson said as he sat and flipped open his spiral notebook to the questions already neatly printed. *Just ease in, Benson. Don't let her get you spooked.* "Can you give me your full name? We want to get it right in the paper. I'm not sure how you spell Nikki." He flashed a quick smile, hoping it would slightly offend her that he didn't have her name memorized.

"Nicole Breanne Harmon. But I go by Nikki, with a *k-k,*" she said with the practiced ease of a statement repeated all her life.

"Well, Nikki with a k-k, I'm going to read the questions, and you just answer the best you can, okay?" He doodled on the paper, feeling eyes bore into his back.

What's Little Ben doing talking to a cheerleader? Someone go push that pussy back into his place. He didn't know if every upper classmen in the cafeteria was thinking it, whispering it to each other, or just puzzling over his mere existence. But he didn't dare look.

"Okay." She leaned forward, much more eager than when she had flipped him off with her ponytail.

Will they come give me a smack down, toss me to the floor? He couldn't stand it, and took a quick glance around him. He had never been the spotlight-hungry Schmidt. When Benson started kindergarten, Colin was already garnering headlines in the Jamestown Daily News. *Eight-year-old Michael Jordan clone in Jamestown* and *Future Michael Vick comfortable in the limelight.*

The coaches bragged on him too, said that "Little Ben" had the same abilities. But the expectations had been through the roof. Colin had a rocket arm and an already polished jump shot. What did Little Ben have?

By the time the youth league got their claws into him, all Little Ben had was a great big chip on his shoulder. He preferred hanging in the shadows of his brother – better to have no attention than feel like a copycat. Especially since he'd never be as good.

But coaches continued to call at the beginning of the city youth leagues every year. No matter how much they asked, he refused to return to the Jamestown Sports Arena. Benson also gave little effort in P.E., except sometimes during the soccer unit. In the middle of first quarter, like clockwork, the P.E. teacher would pull him aside and ask why he didn't try, that it was obvious he had athletic ability. Benson would give an abbreviated version of how much he hated everything sports stood for, that it was a crappy world that let Ray Lewis beat his girlfriend while making millions, yet single mothers all across the country could barely feed their kids. He had practiced the speech often, revising it when a newer athlete got charged with assault. Sometimes he added a quick afterthought about the time it took to keep his honor roll grades.

What teacher could argue with a socially advanced attitude and the importance of grades?

"Benson?" Nikki looked confused by his silence.

"Oh, sorry. Just...just, oh never mind. Okay. Let's get started."

He tapped his pen on the page and asked his first question, writing her answers as fast as he could. He abbreviated, and when the questions got more personal and her responses more emotional, Benson Schmidt felt the noose tightening. And not on him.

When he finished – after she told him to get the hell out of her face – he retreated to a back table to organize his notes, trying to hide his smile. He felt like a third-stringer who threw up a last second shot for the game – and made it.

He turned to a free page in his notebook, not prepared to immortalize it yet in his journal.

Nikki Harmon, 8th grade cheerleader, claimed, "I don't feel we choose our status. It's chosen for us."

Low lifes, she insisted, don't have what it takes to be popular. She wouldn't give details as to what made someone a "low life."

Her answer to, "What makes someone popular?" was a long list: Clothes, friends, willing to take risks, parents' income, attitude, sex appeal, and last but certainly not least, looks.

I pointed out that she had been a nobody until she made the cheerleading squad. She waited a long time before finally agreeing. When asked how she felt about the fragile state of her own popularity, she asked, "What do you mean by fragile?"

I asked her if she didn't make the squad next year when the competition got tougher, did she think she had what it took to be popular without it? Her immediate comeback was, "Don't you think I'm cute enough?"

I just shrugged.

She started crying. The princess may now have a pea of doubt.

Benson smiled. Mrs. Matt wouldn't allow all of it, and she wouldn't approve of the tears.

I'll have to edit my notes before I enter them in my journal. It made him feel sneaky, even a little slimy, but right now, his adrenaline rushed like a flowing volcano. Without losing steam, he marched over and dropped into a seat across from Steve Ralston. His head reeled with what he was doing.

In another world, I would've eaten those spinach-wrapped lima beans before choosing to sit at the same table with Mr. Jock Strap. But with Operation Cappuccino as cover, excitement outweighed the fear.

"I have a proposition for you," he started, trying to remember what he had rehearsed.

"Go back to your rock, runt face." Steve punched numbers into his high-tech calculator, then scrawled something on a page of math calculations. "Christ."

"I could help, if you need it." Benson held his breath. Would he be able to do 9th grade work?

No, but I know someone who can.

"What the hell do you want, retard?" Steve slammed down his pencil and glared at Benson.

"You're one to call someone a retard," a girl at the table behind Steve mumbled.

Benson watched the freshman's face turn so deep red, it had a purple tint. Steve gripped the edge of the table, turned so deliberately, it looked like he might hit her.

"Shut up, Jenni, I don't give a damn what Nikki just said. She's a bitch, anyway. And Megan better watch her mouth, too."

Uh-oh. There's trouble in paradise. His heart beat fast with the possibility that he could chink away at an already existing crack.

Steve turned to face Benson again. "Why're you still here?"

"I'm writing an article for the school paper and an editorial spot in the Jamestown Daily News featuring the elite at Westwood. I guess you don't wanna be part of it." Benson hid his smirk from the mammoth linebacker as he stood to leave.

"Wait! It ain't gonna be an article about the elite if I ain't in it." Steve leaned forward, like he might bite Benson if the urge hit.

Spotlight gets 'em every time.

"That's why I'm asking you, Steve. Even my brother knows you're gonna be a starter next year." Benson flipped the notebook open to a fresh set of questions, adapted for the thick and famous.

"Okay, shoot, penis breath. But if you take too much of my time, you gotta get Laughlin to do my Algebra." Steve cocked an eyebrow, a gesture he must have thought made him look tough. It made Benson want to laugh.

"Okay. First question: If you had to choose just one clique to belong to, which one would it be?"

"That's easy. The studs." Steve turned to see if anyone heard him, but his adoring fans at nearby tables were caught up in other activities.

"That's really what you want me to print? Your parents are gonna read this, moron."

"Who you callin' a moron, Shitty Schmitty? Okay, honest answer. Um, the jocks."

"So you'd be willing to lose the rich boys, the preps, and the cheerleaders? I guess that would count out Megan? You'd have to find a new girlfriend." Benson mimicked Steve's gesture, cocking an eyebrow and sporting a half-grin. He studied the football player's face – square jaw, crooked nose, deep-set brown eyes – all of it jock-typical, except the angry lines creasing his zit-covered forehead.

"The cheerleaders go with the jocks. Kinda like peanut butter and jelly, ya know? Who wants just a jelly sandwich? That's them – not much on their own, but hook 'em up with us, and you got quite a combo. You know, cheerleaders would be nothin' without us," Steve stated matter-of-factly, though quieter than all his other proclamations.

Not macho enough to say that louder, Stevie Poo?

"So without cheerleaders, do you think any *other* girls would like jocks?" This was better than Benson could've dreamed.

"Hey, we're popular 'cause we get attention from the town. Jocks are worshipped. Look at LaDainian, Reggie, even Terrell Owens. Heck, I'm gonna be one of 'em. That spotlight's bright, dude, and I like the heat." The ninth grader sat back, reveling in the imaginary cheers in his mind.

"Those guys are running backs and wide receivers, not offensive linemen. Besides, where would you be if you blew out a knee? Or became a cripple? Do you think people would still like you?" Benson tapped his pencil hard on the tablet covered with his scrawled notes.

Steve didn't answer right away. He picked at a cuticle on his thumb until it bled, his brow knitted in tight lines and his jaw jutted until he looked like he might explode.

"Steve?"

The freshman suddenly slammed an open palm on the table, making Benson and everyone around them jump.

"Stop the damn tapping! God, I don't know. Sports are all I know, man. All my friends are athletes. We been playin' city league since I was seven. You sayin' I wouldn't be popular if I wudn't good at football?" Steve leaned across the table, and Benson thought he might have to scope out an escape route. He made sure he had a clear line of sight with the teacher.

"What would you be popular for, Steve, your brain? Your looks?" Benson's courage amazed even himself.

With everyone but Colin...

"Don't be a smart ass. I'll kick your scrawny butt into next week, you got me?" Steve fidgeted, ready to pounce if Benson agitated him further.

Benson said nothing, but didn't flinch either. He kept his bearings by picturing Mr. Football in twenty years, after the muscle melted to flab. Ralston seemed more buff than ever, his biceps stretching the band on his short-sleeved Polo.

"God, you're such a retard," Steve finally hissed.

"My I.Q.'s way too high for that put-down. Anyway, so you're saying that you'd manhandle people and intimidate them to like you?"

Again, the full-grown teenager sat speechless. At six foot three, two hundred twenty pounds, Steve Ralston, fifteen-year-old star athlete, stared at a seventh grader he'd never spoken to directly in his life except to taunt. He looked on the verge of panic.

For a brief moment, Benson suspected Steve understood what it felt like to be a dreg. Even if it only lasted three minutes.

"I ain't juiced, if that's what you're implying. God. How could someone have such a cool brother and be such a damn *geek*? Get outta my face, Schmidt. I got work to do." Steve grabbed his binder and unzipped it so fast, papers spewed out onto the table. On top lay a note with Megan's name signed with hearts and curly-cues. But block letters had been scratched over the entire note with enough force to rip the paper. Benson's mouth fell open, seeing the word *bitch* scrawled on the page.

And who the heck brought up juicing?

Benson had watched ESPN enough to know what it meant, especially after Conseco wrote a book about it. He felt an unexpected wave of pity for the jock. But he didn't let it sway his determination. He hustled to his corner seat to rewrite Steve's answers. He wouldn't worry about Mrs. Matt's censoring or disapproval yet, because his best friend would give it a huge thumb's up.

His smug grin had to puzzle the preps as they watched him walk around the cafeteria making a chart of who sat where. The blueprint would serve as his recipe for success, and he would stir in each ingredient, one at a time.

Benson's Interview Notes

Hey, Ryan – here are quick notes from my interviews...
thought I'd write them in our project binder so we can go back
to them and not forget stuff.

Nikki Harmon – Made her cry, realizes she's only popular
'cause she's a cheerleader.

Steve Ralston – *Really* exposed some nerves for Mr. Jock...
he called Nikki a bitch! Gave me the best line ever...he said
cheerleaders would "be nothing without jocks." Hmmm. That
may come in handy.

Evan Anderson – Only asked one question, but after Steve
said that about cheerleaders, I wanted to know if another jock
agreed. He *didn't*, can you believe it? Said Ralston had *way*
bigger issues than his mouth...what the heck does that mean?

Jenni Waterman – didn't plan to interview her, so I didn't
have set questions. But I wanted to know what was going on
between her and Steve...guess what? She said Steve and Megan
were on the outs! That Steve is "so 5 minutes ago." Wow!

Pam Utterbeck – Fun interviewing a friend...she wants us to
call her Goth Girl in the project to protect the guilty. ☺ I asked
if Steve was right (about cheerleaders). Her response: "In ten
years, they'll have beer bellies, boring jobs, and be livin' in the
glory days about when they were somebody. This is their only
time to shine, Benson. Don't spoil their fun. Gives them fuel
for therapy in a few years."

Note: Malakai didn't want to be interviewed...said Steve knew
everything and could speak for all jocks.

Steve Ralston's Note

Megan,

we gotta talk. I've had a crappy day, and now u r not talking 2 me. what's ↑? god, what a lousy freaking day. and i did NOT call you a bitch. whoever told u that is a liar. jenni and allison both dogged me during study hall, but i never said jack about YOU, i swear. please let me make it up to u. i need to hold u, kiss u, and well, u know. PLEAZE give me a chance. not seeing you these past 5 weekends has killed me, and everybodys saying u r breaking up with me. is that true?

god, if it is, i'll just kill myself. i can't live without u. 4 real.

please write back. i love u, in case u 4-got. I'll apologize everyday for the rest of my life for all the shit I've done. I swear I will.

LYL

Steve

Chapter 5

THE AFTER-SCHOOL halls buzzed as Benson dialed his locker combination. He wished Ryan hadn't ditched him for a tutoring session with Ms. Waters at lunch and after school, but they planned to meet at his house to go over their notes. That would finally give him a chance to share the interviews.

"Who knew Ralston could be such an idiot? Dissing cheerleaders. What a moron," a girl to his right was saying as she reached into her locker and swapped books for a sweater and her purse.

"I got the 411 on the whole thing," another Barbie said, nodding her ponytail.

Benson flipped through his textbooks, pretending to consider which to take home. He got most of his homework finished during class, which was a good thing since he used his study hall for interviews. But for the sake of hearing more, he stalled.

"That idiot called her a bitch. Can you believe that?" A letter-jacketed guy threw everything inside his locker and slammed it before things could fall out. "Guy's planning to be celibate for a while. The juice has gone to his brain, for real."

The rumor mill had brewed all day, and every conversation seemed to be about the same thing. Benson's stomach stewed.

There's that word again...do junior high guys really do that crap? He'd like to ask Colin, but that ranked right up there with eating lima beans and boogers.

"Yeah, and it ain't all he's dipping his finger into, I hear," the first girl said, slamming her locker closed.

Man, if I started this, Mrs. Matt's gonna kill us.

Before he could get his backpack zipped, kids slammed into him, knocking him against his locker. "God! Get off m..."

"FIGHT!" The word erupted down the student-packed hall

like a spewing volcano, clearing a school faster than a fire alarm. The wave of frenzied energy sent Benson to his knees scrambling for his books. He clamored to his feet and barely avoided being gouged by the corner of his locker door still standing open. Nothing could be heard over the din of pounding feet and shouts. As soon as there was a break in the pack, he plunged into the mass and had to jog to keep from being stampeded.

"FIGHT IN THE CIRCLE DRIVE! C'MON!" the throng repeated like a rippling tide. The instant the swarm of students staggered out the doors by the circle drive, everyone fell dead silent.

"You're a jerk, Steve!" a girl shouted, though Benson could see no faces.

Backpacks and papers littered the sidewalk where people had dropped their stuff. Buses lined the drive in front of Westwood, but no one sat inside them because all the action was in front of the main school doors. Scores of students crowded the area. Benson weaseled through them until he found a stone bench and stepped up onto it.

His heart tripped in his chest to see Steve squared off against a blonde – Megan Barker. Next to her was another boy, a freshman who hung out with his brother every once in a while. Benson couldn't think of his name. *They all sorta look alike...*

The three shouted until veins popped out on their necks, Megan with tears streaming down her cheeks. A teacher would interrupt the confrontation any second, so the crowd closed in tighter around them, like a protective shell.

"Shut up, Megan. You're such a slut – *you* know what you did. Should I tell all of 'em?" Steve Ralston waved his hands to the ogling mass.

Oh, God. Benson's head spun with the possibility of being the catalyst. He refused to accept that one tiny interview could spark all this. *There was trouble way before now...Jenni's comment proved that.* Ralston had absolutely called his girlfriend the "b" word...at least on paper.

"I'm gonna beat the crap outta you, Ralston." Spittle flew

from the blond guy's mouth, more veins popping out on his forehead as his head shook with rage. He yanked off his letter jacket with methodical jerks, then threw it to the ground.

The crowd roared approval, the impact of that gesture clear.

"Hit him, Michael!" someone growled.

That's it! Michael Barker – Megan's brother – he's in the paper almost as much as Colin.

"Bring it, Barker! C'mon!" Steve tossed his own jacket to the sidewalk, a smug look on his flushed face. The three of them were the hub in a wheel of students, shielded from teachers. He fought the urge to go get someone, but he knew better. That would cost more than a black eye or two.

"STOP!" Megan screamed, then put her hands over her face like she was going to have a breakdown.

"That jerk called your sister a *bitch!*" a student screamed.

Others echoed encouragement, trying to trigger punches, the crowd hyped for blood.

Some girl beside Benson whispered to her friend. "Steve and Michael used to be tight, like best friends. What happened?"

Best friends? Then the first punch landed, the sickening sound of fist to face. Nothing Hollywood, but a smack that sprayed blood from Steve's lip, then Michael's nose. Megan screamed again for them to stop, but their put-downs volleyed back and forth with such venom, they couldn't hear her. Or chose not to.

The crowd encouraged the hysteria, chanting, "Hit him! Hit him! Hit him!" Probably for the first time in his near-adult life, Steve Ralston was on the wrong side of the cheering section.

The more everyone screamed, the more Benson's head reeled – the shouting, the weight of what it meant, the cool breeze that should've been refreshing if the world hadn't been so screwed up.

Just when it seemed impossible to stop, teachers swooped in by the handful.

"Break it up! Now!" they ordered, parting the crowd like Moses.

Everyone scattered backward, acting bewildered by what their classmates were capable of. A few looked dazed, like they had just woken from a bad dream.

"Did Megan break up with him?" one of the girls beside him yelled, barely able to be heard over the commotion. Two teachers wedged themselves between Steve Ralston and Michael Barker, who guarded his little sister. Steve's bloody lip had puffed up already, and his mussed hair added to the psychotic effect. Michael rubbed his bruised knuckles.

"I'll get you, Ralston, I swear to God." Michael, pushed back by Mr. Drysdale, the assistant principal, spit in Steve's direction.

Megan burst into fresh tears, gibbering about jocks and their egos. "Get a girlfriend now, Steven. See if you can," she yelled, then mumbled something else. But everyone was already oohing and ahhing over what she had said. The inference was clear. *Without cheerleaders and their friends, who else would jocks date?*

Titters from the crowd angered Steve. His face turned fiery red, as he was led toward the circle drive doors and the office. Benson hoped Mrs. Matt wouldn't nix their project because of the fight. Would she think their interviews caused this mess? Benson didn't know, because he wasn't sure yet himself.

"God, what a jerk. I hope no cheerleader ever dates him," some girl yelled in Steve's direction, then took Megan by the arm. The cheerleader or closely related species swept her hair back like she was at a Hollywood audition.

Benson cringed. *They'd be nothin' without us...* Isn't that what Steve had said?

Mr. Baillargeon, a young social studies teacher everybody liked, shooed students onto buses. Mrs. Mattingly stood at the door like a prison guard, motioning first Michael inside, then Steve.

People booed Steve as it shut behind him.

"I hate you!" Megan screamed at the door. She wiped viciously at the tears running down her cheeks. The crowd hissed with gossip, riders clamoring onto buses, walkers wandering in various directions, athletes hustling to get to practice.

You'll be missing a few key guys, Benson wanted to tell them.

He planned to walk the mile and a half to Ryan's, so he dawdled by the stone benches outlining the circle drive, waiting for everything to clear so he could retrieve his book bag. He ached to say something to Megan, not that he would in a million years. But it didn't stop him from staring.

A split second later, Steve came barreling out the door. The two-hundred-pound football player looked like he was going for a game-saving sack.

Benson's mouth fell open, his heart leaping into his throat.

"CATCH HIM!" Mr. Baillargeon ordered, as Ralston pummeled a couple of students in his beeline for Megan.

Mrs. Mattingly, still standing guard at the door, turned so fast that Steve slammed right into her. The remaining crowd gasped. Mrs. Matt gripped his shoulders like a parent scolding a toddler, even though Steve stood nearly a head taller. He raised his arms inside hers like he meant to break free, his glare at Megan making his intent too clear. But the freshman basketball coach cutting him off diffused his plan.

"Stop it, Steve Ralston. Get hold of yourself right now, or you won't play football the rest of the season, do you hear me?" Mrs. Matt's gritted teeth and her tone made Benson's insides flip. When Steve twitched, Mrs. Mattingly took another step sideways to keep herself between him and his target. The coach did the same.

Mr. Drysdale raced out the door, obviously in pursuit of his escapee, furious blotches of red on each cheek. The assistant principal grabbed Steve and shoved him backward, pinning the freshman to the brick building while barking orders into his walkie-talkie. Benson couldn't see Mr. Drysdale's face now, but the trembling hands and ruthless hold said plenty.

"You just keep making it worse." Mr. Drysdale turned Steve toward the door and growled at the bystanders. "Go home. *Now.*"

Mouths hung open, people too stunned to speak. Several cheerleaders gawked at Steve in disgust. His position on the food chain had plummeted, and the jock knew it. Benson could see it in Steve's eyes every time he glared at Megan.

"Show's over. Go on, get home." Mr. Baillargeon shooed the remaining kids away, buzzing about the fight.

Different versions spawned faster than Barbie Brigade gossip. Benson even heard a girl say she couldn't believe Steve had punched his girlfriend in the face. *Was she watching the same fight?*

Someone grabbed Benson's arm from behind. "What the f—?"

"Yo, Benson, what happened here? God, I miss everything." Ryan scrubbed a hand over his unruly red hair.

"You scared the crap outta me, Ryan. Don't do that." Benson's heart hammered from being startled, the fight, the past two days of stress.

"Sorry, man. What happened?"

Benson gave an abbreviated, unembellished version, replaying the fight while he made Ryan help him retrieve his books and backpack. He had to pause after nearly every detail to answer a question until he finally whacked Ryan on the arm.

"Ow." Ryan tossed Benson's math book back inside their locker.

"Stop being such a weenie, Ryan, and let me finish. I think I caused this." Benson found the last of his things, and they headed back out the same circle drive doors toward Ryan's house.

"For real?"

"Yeah. I interviewed Steve today, and he said cheerleaders would be nothing without jocks. I, uh, might've repeated that to two or three people, seeing as Megan is, or *was*, his girlfriend." Benson looked over both shoulders like a spy checking his cover as they crossed through the teacher parking lot. "I wouldn't have done it if I'd thought..." But he couldn't finish. He was sure everyone knew what he had done, and the burning sensation in his stomach had suddenly been stirred with icicles.

They wound past Westwood Junior High and made their way around the giant practice field where the three football squads ran drills. Whistles came from different directions. The freshman team jogged along the perimeter's track, the eighth graders ran a play in the middle, and the seventh graders did calisthenics off to the side.

"Oh, man, look." Benson pointed to the far end where the ninth grade quarterbacks were throwing bullets to receivers.

Evan Anderson and Kevin Smiley, normally lined up side by side as wide outs on the scrimmage line, stood nose-to-nose with veins bulging and spittle flying. They shouted, their heads going up and down like bobble-heads.

"SHUT UP!" Evan screamed. But the rest of the heated exchange couldn't be deciphered. Benson and Ryan, at least fifty yards away, understood the body language of the bobbing heads.

Kevin jabbed at Evan's shoulder pads. Evan slammed his hands into Smiley's, and the two were locked in a death grip until one of the coaches barked an indiscernible order. In seconds, both were side by side doing push-ups.

Benson couldn't understand a word the players or the coach had said, but there was no doubt in his mind what the guys were arguing about.

Some things were becoming clearer to him as Operation Cappuccino gathered steam – popularity wasn't based on quality of friends but quantity.

If the project worked, they intended to turn *that* kind of thinking around.

Megan Barker's Notes

Steve,

I can't believe you had the nerve to call me a slut. I've told my parents almost everything, and as much as they loved you before, they will hate you just as much as I do. Don't come near me or my friends ever again. And I can guarantee you'll never date another cheerleader... you'll have to go over to Parkway to find girls, unless they have already found out the kind of guy you really are. Maybe you should consider a boyfriend.

All this talk about killing yourself is just as cruel as everything else you've done. And if you retaliate, I will tell. Do you understand? I WILL TELL.

Megan

Benson's Journal

Thursday, September 18th

    After Ryan and I worked on the project at his house, I got home right after Colin, and Mrs. Matt, he was totally certifiable. I tried to provoke him, even called him a jerk. But nothing worked. When I mentioned the rough day I'd had...about the fight (I won't tell him about the interviews because he's friends with all those...preps), he went ballistic. Really started screaming at me to get the f--- out of his face and why the hell did I have to always be around.

    He's usually in a good mood after football practice, and I think I should've reminded him that I live here too.

    Mrs. Matt, did you have brothers or sisters? Did you ever want to help them but hate them all at the same time?

    They're so complicated. I wonder if he knows Steve will probably be suspended and Westwood will blow the winning streak his class started. Hard to say whether that'll tick him off or make him want to throw a party. He's just confusing in general, and even though he hangs with a lot of those guys, I don't think he likes them too much.

    I wonder if Colin and Steve are friends... I think

I'll ask him at dinner. After what Steve did today, he's going to need all he can get.

Chapter 6

FRIDAY AT WESTWOOD Junior High was electric. Because of the fight and the repeated slurs, a wedge had been driven between most of the athletes and cheerleaders. Benson couldn't wait to see the dynamics at lunch. Before school, he heard several versions of why Steve and Michael hadn't been suspended.

Benson wasn't surprised – the privileged didn't live by the same rules as the rest of them. In a weird way, he was relieved. He felt guilty enough for the fight without the weight of Westwood's record on the line.

A bunch of them congregated by lockers outside the cafeteria, a hangout for those who didn't eat breakfast at school.

"One measly day of ISD! Can you get over that garbage?" Tim Silvey smirked. Benson had heard his former neighbor rant about "kiddie prison" enough to recite the protests.

The tattooed seventh grader, taller and skinnier than most, compared in-school detention to kissing his sister. But he admitted he got more work done in ISD. "Who learns that much at school?" he griped.

"If it wasn't football season, it'd be different. But our freshmen are undefeated. The ninth grade coaches haven't lost a game in two years, thanks to Colin's class." Ryan added some statistics that made Benson want to vomit. Instead, he whopped his best friend on the arm.

"I bet if that had been me, my ass'd be at home. ISD, pshht. Whoever heard of a lousy day of ISD when punches are thrown? And everybody knows the jerk is on steroids. No fifteen-year-old grows muscles like that over the summer." Tim furrowed his dark brow, tossed a notebook in the bottom of his locker, and grabbed a binder.

Benson shrugged, not wanting to offer his take on it – first offenses and all the things his parents said at the dinner table the night before. And, if the steroid rumor *was* true, Steve would be in custody, not in ISD, right? Of course, his dad had a different opinion.

Benson had swallowed a bite of pork chop and added, "Can you believe Ralston did all that?" He eyed Colin, who'd said absolutely nothing since dinner started.

"Boys should be cut some slack. They're under a lot of pressure," his dad had said, swirling wine in his glass. "I'm not saying what Steve did was right, but it's his first offense, I'm sure. And there's no way a junior high kid is on steroids. Please."

Colin had brooded through the entire meal, offering no comments, not even when his dad directly asked for his oldest son's opinion. Thinking about it now, Benson couldn't remember a time his brother hadn't had one.

He'd even gone to Colin's room after dinner, mustering the guts to ask if he'd been friends with Ralston. But the door was locked, and when he tapped, Colin snapped, "Go away!"

At breakfast, Colin said nothing, ate nothing, and had done even less to get ready for school. His mom suggested he stay home, and he shocked the whole family by agreeing. Colin hadn't missed a day of school in four years.

Standing in the hall outside his first hour class, Benson listened to Tim rant...if nothing, his friend kept it all in perspective.

"Jocks play by different rules, and that's why they all grow up to be principals...so they can continue the crap-on-the-little-guy cycle. Tell me I'm wrong." Tim glared from Benson to Pam to Ryan.

"You didn't think Drysdale would ruin our chance at winning regional championships, didja?" Ryan gave a sarcastic chuckle. "We're not all equal. We know that better than anybody."

Benson nodded. He'd learned that lesson at home, some days worse than others.

"Well, it sucks to be me." Tim straightened the silver post

in his eyebrow almost as if the conversation reminded him he
was different. Most of the time, he preferred it that way.

But Benson knew a hothead like Steve Ralston – as long as
the jock channeled most of his aggression on the football field
– would get a wrist slap for his mistakes.

"Get outta my way, Benson," Nikki Harmon hissed as she
fought her way through Tim, Benson, and Ryan, on her way to
Cheerleader Corner.

"Sure," Benson muttered, having lost his quick-witted
tongue from study hall. He was floored she remembered his
name.

"Hey, Nikki!" another cheerleader shouted down the hall,
racing past them.

"Barbie crossing," Tim muttered as he stomped off to class.

The Blue Jay skirt flipped up and down as Barbie jogged
down the hall, ribbons and ponytail bopping as she went. "You
hear about Megan and Steve? After the fight yesterday, she..."
Several other girls clamored around the two cheerleaders,
lowering their voices to gossip.

Benson didn't know Barbie's real name, but he strained to
hear her as he stuffed morning materials into his backpack.

"See you in a minute. I need Ms. Water's help with one of
my math problem," Ryan marched down the hall, oblivious of
the gossip gutter.

Benson grinned. *Needed* was a relative term, but if Ms.
Waters had time, Ryan would make up a reason to be there.
And without the threat of Ralston intercepting him, he didn't
need an escort.

An undercurrent pulsed through the halls of Westwood,
renditions of what had happened morphing faster than melt-
ing ice cream.

"I know, and I heard Megan is pressing charges for him
hitting her..."

"And she should! What about Steve slapping Mrs. Matt and
not getting suspended? I mean, *come on!*"

Slapping Mrs. Matt? Are they for real?

Benson studied each cheerleader's expression. He would
add all this to Operation Cappuccino's response sheets. *Thank*

God I witnessed the fight, or I wouldn't know what the heck to believe.

The Barbie Brigade finally headed to class, only minutes before the bell, and little else happened the rest of the morning. During second hour, Benson and Ryan didn't get finished with their questions in time to get them approved by Mrs. Mattingly. Not that they tried too hard. They wouldn't be interviewing anyone today. *Wait for the dust to settle,* they both agreed. And they worried about Mrs. Matt's reaction to the interviews anyway. She had read through their next set of questions, initialed the new entries, then left them to be picked up on their way out of class.

Not having a face-to-face with her suited Benson just fine.

"After the weekend, all this'll die down. Don't you think?" Benson raised his eyebrows and accepted Ryan's *sure*, even if his gut didn't agree.

By lunch, it was clear Operation Cappuccino and whatever else brewed in the Westwood hallways had turned their world upside down. When they met to go into the cafeteria together – too uncertain to face it alone – neither could have prepared for it.

No one sat in the same place. Strangely, most didn't sit at all. A few jocks paired up with cheerleaders, and several members of the freshman football team kept returning to the lunch line for seconds and thirds of chicken nuggets. But most of their classmates milled about like hurricane survivors – lost, displaced, confused.

"Look," Ryan said, pointing at the empty tables at the front, the three elite tables. Evan Anderson, jock extra-ordinaire leaned against a locker next to Tim Silvey. Each munched on a sandwich and gabbed about a neighbor whose home had burned down. The two lived only a few houses apart, but worlds had separated them when Evan sprouted muscles and Tim only developed attitude.

Oh, my God. Benson wanted to smile, wanted to relish what was happening, but it felt weird – wrong even, in light of how it happened.

He scanned the room, ears catching a political debate, but

Benson's mouth fell open when he saw who was having it.

Malakai Jeffries, phenom running back, sat backwards on a seat talking with Pam Utterbeck at the next table. Her goth style made her stand out just as much as his football jersey. They debated the upcoming election with friendly fervor, getting heated about liberals running for president, shocking Benson that either had an opinion about it. Megan Barker came from the juice station and offered her two cents' worth, insisting that a middle-of-the-road, non-partisan candidate had the only true answers to America's problems. Malakai sparked more debate when he pledged his vote for the *right* gender. "We're not ready for PMS in the White House. I mean, that other dude smoked pot in high school...he can't be all bad."

Pam argued that it might be time for the U.S. to finally elect a woman, even if she was radical. Who else could sift through all the crap men had made of things?

Benson laughed, astounded that Megan even knew what *non-partisan* meant. His parents talked politics frequently, so he picked up things, but Megan "blonder than Jessica Simpson" Barker?

I guess she has parents, too.

They stood watching too long to have time to eat or to weave to the back of the cafeteria for a place to sit. When the bell rang, they hustled down the hall gabbing about what it all meant, and then finally headed to their fifth hour classes.

The rest of the afternoon, rumors festered. By the end of the day, Benson couldn't believe how much the whole thing had snowballed.

"I gotta see Ms. Waters real quick – getting replacement papers for the Algebra stuff I lost during the fight. Drop this in the locker, wouldja? And then I'll see you at my house by three-thirty, okay?" Ryan handed Benson a social studies textbook and headed toward their math class.

"Sure," Benson said. He raced to the locker, excited by the prospect of refining Operation Cappuccino for the first section that was due Monday. They'd show Mrs. Matt the upside of what they had uncovered, not just the exposed nerves.

He dropped Ryan's book on the top shelf and stooped to fill his backpack. Other students slammed lockers all around him, while two freshmen jabbered about the high school game against Parkway – Colin's first appearance in front of scouts from Notre Dame – and where the best parties were afterward.

He wondered how they knew, a twinge of jealousy rippling through him. Was this how Colin always felt? Part of the inner circle? Shaking it off, he caught a glimpse of the Barbie Brigade gathered at the end of the hall. Cheerleader Corner, some referred to it, but Ryan called it The Hot Spot – where all the cheerleaders shared various lockers and congregated every day so the entire student body could get a good view for worship services.

Benson's ears pricked when he heard Steve's name spat out of someone's mouth like spoiled milk. Crouching still, he sorted through the slew of papers in the bottom and continually side-glanced the band of girls.

Whispers, low, incoherent hisses, tickled his ears. They fueled his new journalistic curiosity. When the hallway cleared a little, he tuned in to their conversation, catching little bits here and there.

"I don't...another...as long as I live. Screw him. Or...*don't.*"

Several girls coughed laughter. Benson knew a few of their names and thought most were eighth grade cheerleaders. *I guess you only mingle with the nobodies at lunch.*

The last few stragglers wandered out, leaving the hallway empty and better than a microphone.

"C'mon, Megan. Guys are such posers. They just do it to look macho. You could forgive him, ya know."

"Forgive him? For what he did? His damn image is more important than how I feel. You really think we're nothing without jocks? I mean, *really?* Please." Megan shook her ponytail, then threw the last of her stuff in a locker.

"She doesn't need that idiot anyway. Tell 'em about your new guy, Megan," Nikki prompted. Megan shot her a look. Benson saw the exchange and wondered if the Brigade had pairings that were tighter than the whole.

"You can't believe how much more mature high school

guys are. Not all guys good at sports are jocks. He took me to that big party last weekend, and he didn't try to make moves on me the whole time." Megan added something else in a whisper that Benson couldn't hear.

One girl shook her head, another giggled, but most stood with their hands on their hips. Benson had seen a lot of Megan Barker, Lisa Kincheloe rode his bus, and he had firsthand experience with Nikki Harmon. Jenni Waterman, the girl Steve had ticked off just before Benson interviewed him, was by far the snottiest, though Nikki ran a close second. He didn't know the rest by name except Allison, who was in a couple of his classes. He memorized faces so he could get Colin's freshman yearbook and look them up. These things mattered now.

"I'm sorry, any guy who thinks a girl is nothing without him – *he's* the nothing. Steve and I were finished anyway... And you girls need to stay away from him. He's too damn horny."

More giggles erupted from the Corner. Benson watched them as he messed around with papers, shoving a few in his backpack. The words ebbed and flowed like a receding tide, driving him crazy. He could hear better when he watched their mouths.

When have I ever cared what these people were saying? What the hell do I care if Megan snotty shoes breaks up with Studman Steve? And she's already got a new man? Jesus, does this girl ever do homework?

"But, God, Megan, you saw him going out to ISD this morning. I felt sorry for him. He's been my friend since second grade."

Benson studied the girl's expression. Her auburn hair framed her plump face, and he could sense her uncertainty at speaking out against her friends. He didn't know her, but staring at her skewered his insides. She hadn't gone to Field Elementary with most of them. Or if she had, she hadn't been as beautiful.

"Michael's told everyone about Steve pushing me." Megan dropped her head. "Guys think he's a coward for it, and girls think he's a jerk. He did it to himself, Mallorie. And that's not all anyway. He...he...let's just say that whatever Steve gets, he *deserves*."

Mallorie...

"What're you looking at, Benson?"

Before he realized it, one of the girls stared straight at him, her arms crossed and her top lip curled in disgust. The whole circle turned on him like a pack of gossip-starved preps.

"Nothing," he mumbled, throwing the remaining note-books into the bottom of his locker. He grabbed his book bag and raced down the opposite hall trying not to hear the degrading comments chasing him.

"God, what a moron," Nikki said, loud enough for him to hear as he turned the corner.

"Ya know, his brother is hot, and he's so – *strange*."

He wanted to look back to see who said that, but he didn't dare. He paused at the corner, out of sight. He ached to bolt, but he had thrown his interview journal in his locker. He had to have it for their project plans.

"He's sorta cute though. Why does he hang out with that dork Ryan? God, *he* can really get on your nerves," added Mallorie, the girl at the top of his yearbook-hunting list.

The girls continued to talk as they meandered out a side door. Benson peeked around the corner when it sounded like the coast was clear. He couldn't deny that the encounter embarrassed him, and catching bits of their harsh remarks renewed his fervor to dethrone the royal snobs.

They don't know a damn thing about me. Benson's blood boiled when he hit the side doors and sprinted almost the entire way to Ryan's house. It would be an afternoon of major planning for the two of them – and a weekend to perfect it.

Benson bounded up the stairs to his best friend's room. In a matter of minutes, charts lay scattered and strewn about on a desk now cleared of peace signs. He noticed the sun-bleached outline of absent stickers. Closet doors once covered now looked naked without them. Benson wanted to tell Ryan to at least replace them with something, but he couldn't imagine what his friend would choose. Pictures of Einstein or Bill Gates?

"Holy crap, Benson, this rocks!" Ryan smacked Benson's hands in a high ten when they finished.

They laughed, drained the last of their Dr Peppers, and settled in front of Ryan's Play Station. An hour of innocent fun refreshed Benson. The dirty feeling from his after-school encounter finally passed, but it was one he would feel again.

Soon.

Ryan's Journal

Sunday, September 21st

Benson and I outlined notes all weekend and finally got our first part ready to turn in. We badgered Colin until he shoveled some dirt on Steve, and there was a ton of stuff I had forgotten. Like the tantrums Steve used to throw, even kicked Malakai's butt in 4th grade, and they are like really good friends. Except Colin said they didn't become chummy until Steve could get past Mal being black. And the next year, Steve shoved a hot dog up a new kid's nose. I'd heard that one but never knew if it was really true. When Colin was in sixth grade, Steve got "rubber band happy" and popped Colin in the leg. Colin didn't share specifics, but he said Ralston learned his lesson about messing with an upperclassman. Hard to think of a 6th grader as an upperclassman, but whatever.

Benson and I decided that athletes get away with bullying. It's the natural order of things, like Darwinism or something.

Why is it that jocks like to rough up the underdog though? It can't make them feel macho, can it? Benson said they just like to perform, and dogging a little kid is good practice. He griped about Colin using him during every season, how the *teasing and pecking changed depending on the sport. I don't really know why Colin picks on him, or if Benson blows it out of proportion, because when he talks about Colin in private, you can tell he has a little Colin-envy. He can deny it, but his brother's a cool guy when he wants to be.*

I can't decide why Colin's a jerk when no one's around. I've witnessed some brutal battles between them. Is that the real Colin or just part of some twisted pre-game routine?

I wish I had a brother. Better to be a tackling dummy than alone, I think. But I guess, in a way, Bennie is. A brother, I mean.

Benson's Journal

Sunday, September 21st

We kicked butt on our assignment, Mrs. Matt. You're going to be so proud of us. Get this – Colin actually talked with us about stuff. Ryan wanted the scoop on Steve, and for once, my brother didn't completely blow us off. I'd deny it if anybody told him, but it was really cool to just talk with him like a regular guy.

Anyway, tomorrow's the big day. I have interview notes to get approved, we turn in part one, and we'll see if the gossip settled over the weekend.

Plenty of drama right here at home. Colin had a date Saturday night and wouldn't tell us who with. And that's two or three weekends in a row. Some girl called that afternoon, and she asked for Colin. I wanted to ask who was calling sooooo bad. But I knew I'd take crap for a week if I did. Not worth the Indian torture or pink belly. I asked Colin who it was, but he wouldn't tell me, just said it was some girl he was going out with. No biggie, he claimed. But he sure spent a long time in the bathroom for it being 'No biggie.'

He's so cool one minute, then Cocky Colin the next. I hope I'm not

so weird when I go to high school. He was late
getting home and got in trouble. Not exactly
grounded, Dad said, but couldn't go out next
Friday AND Saturday...ooooh, that'll cramp his
style. What will the cruise route do without him?

I think Dad went easy because Colin played so
great Friday night. All Mom and Dad could talk
about at dinner tonight was Colin this, Colin that.
Gag me with a shovel, wouldja? Three touchdown
passes, thanks to great catches by Jase. Scrambled
for over a hundred yards, scored on the game-
winning drive. Dad acted like he'd done it himself.
Makes me feel like a visitor in my own house, (but it
was a great game). Ryan and I went, but this time
we sat behind my parents, nowhere near Larry the
Loser or any of the pep rally boneheads.

That game-winning drive was something, but
why does Dad relive it all the time? I mean, what's
the point? To drive me crazy?

It's working.

Maybe I'll win the George Polk Award and...
And what? No scouts are going to call the house
and ask to visit with me, like Notre Dame did.
They're coming again next Saturday to talk with
Colin. He's a freaking sophomore. Why are they in
such a hurry?

He'll be impossible all week now. I may never
survive it.

Chapter 7

BENSON THOUGHT MONDAY would bring a fresh week and a fresh start.

He was wrong. He didn't see the second fight – the blow-up in the cafeteria while everyone ate breakfast – but he felt the aftermath. Anger pulsed in the halls like a rabid animal, suspensions now imminent and a football team divided in its wake.

Racing to his locker, Benson grabbed his math book and jetted to class. He had overslept, and Colin had been less than thrilled about dropping him off at school. At least his brother hadn't demanded the usual four or five dollars for gas money, obviously distracted by something but bailing on the opportunity to take it out on Benson. Colin wouldn't forget the favor though. He kept a list above his driver's side visor.

"Yo, Ryan, what the heck happened this morning?" Benson hurried into his seat just before the bell and whipped out his math homework.

"They got into it right in the middle of the cafeteria! While everyone was eating breakfast... *Bam*!" Ryan smacked his fist into his other palm. "Steve just plowed into Megan's brother and started beating the crap out of him. Had Michael down pounding on him. Took three teachers to get Steve off him."

"Okay, boys, no more fight talk. Homework, class, let's trade and grade." Ms. Waters, who ranked right up there with Mrs. Matt in the likeability and looks department, meant business when the bell rang. The class passed their assignments backward, a well-oiled machine at work.

"Dang. I can't believe I missed it," Benson murmured. Several others were passing notes and trying to fill in the details of what had become the hottest drama to hit Westwood so far this year.

Ryan whispered, "Mr. Drysdale practically threw Ralston down. Then he got *so* ticked at all the kids watching, I thought he was gonna pop a vessel. Called for Dr. Jacobsen, and that's the first time I've *ever* seen the principal mad." Ryan waited while Ms. Waters brought the papers from the back row to the front. When she started going through the answers, Ryan jotted on a scrap paper, recounting the assistant principal's lecture, and how he threatened every one of the spectators with lunch detention, while Dr. Jacobsen took Steve and Michael to the office.

Ms. Waters grabbed the last note from Benson's hand and dropped it in the trash, scowling at them. They bowed their heads and weathered the wait. The bell finally rang, and Ryan picked up right where he left off while they filled their backpacks.

"Mr. Drysdale used the coolest line, and I think we need to put it in our project." Ryan lowered his voice an octave. *"Take out your mirror before you get out your magnifying glass."* They hustled to their locker. "Isn't that cool?"

"Downright chilly," Benson agreed, trying not to laugh. He loved Ryan's energy but couldn't match it yet. He was still tired from oversleeping.

"Aaand..." Ryan paused, opened their locker, then stared at Benson with a smirk on his face.

"And? What else?" Benson raised his eyebrows. "Better news than that?"

They both tossed their math books inside and gathered spiral notebooks and the outline for Operation Cappuccino.

"Maybe. Depends what you think would be *better*." Ryan slammed the locker and led the way toward Publications.

"Well, give it up." Benson had to speed-walk to keep up, which meant Ryan was practically running.

"Guess who went out with Megan Saturday night?" He slowed to let Benson catch up, his enormous smile scrunching his nose and every single freckle.

"Well, how the heck should I know?" They both stopped outside Mrs. Matt's room.

Meet in the Media Center for class today, a sign on the

door read. They turned toward the stairs and hustled up them to get to class on time.

"You should," Ryan said, turning to his best friend, grinning wickedly. The expression sent Benson's heart racing.

"What?" Then it clicked. Colin's mysterious date, the phone call. "Nuh-uh. No way, Ryan, no way, man. You're making this up." Suddenly, his worlds raced down the same track, headed straight toward one another. Someone had questioned his motives of stirring the very waters in which his brother swam. Now he understood the dangers. A girl's backpack whipped inches from his face as they reached the top of the stairs.

"Yep, the one and only. She showed up with several friends to a sophomore party Saturday night, and she and Colin spent the whole evening arm in arm, caught up totally in each other. Rumor has it they made google eyes all night long. And guess what?"

"Just tell me. God, you're killing me." His stomach suddenly hurt worse than the time he had food poisoning.

"Lighten up, dude." Ryan slowed. They both knew Mrs. Matt would be lenient about a tardy since class had been moved for the day. "Megan's wearing Colin's letter jacket this morning. I saw her, and I asked her how she got it."

"You're kidding. She's wearing my brother's letter jacket? And *you* talked to her?" Benson's mouth fell open. He didn't know which blew his mind more. "Colin treats that jacket better than his autographed Ken Griffey bat." *Or me. But that goes without saying.*

"Yep. Well, she totally blew me off, but can you believe it? No offense, but Colin is about as jock as you can get. She's got a double standard. One minute she's preaching at that fight about not needing some dumb football player, and the next she's dating the biggest jock in Jamestown."

"Shut up," Benson snapped, hard enough to let his best friend know it ticked him off. *No matter how much I hate him, he's still my brother.*

"Sorry. Don't get your panties in a bunch. You hate Colin more than fractions, and you suck at fractions." Ryan took a step back and frowned at Benson.

The look on his best friend's face squeezed his insides in an invisible fist, but he held a hand up and shook his head. "But he is *not* Steve Jockstrap. Colin's an athlete, but he's not a *dumb jock*. He's a straight A student, Ryan, and really, he isn't all that cocky." He started to add *except with me,* but he didn't. It bordered on eating lima beans defending Colin, but comparing him to Steve felt all wrong.

"Well, whatever." Ryan was annoyed. Benson could tell by the arch in his eyebrows. "All I know is she'll be too good for any junior high guy now."

The tardy bell rang, and both of them jogged down the long hall that led to the cafeteria in one direction, the Media Center in the other. Benson couldn't process all of it. Colin dating a junior high girl?

"Sorry, man, I didn't mean to bite your head off," Benson said as he jerked the Media Center door open.

Ryan grabbed his head, like he was making sure it was still attached. "It's still here. I didn't mean to make you mad. But it doesn't really fit. You'd have thought she would've gone brainiac or something. You know, extremes. She *needs* a guy like *me.*" Ryan grinned. Their class was milling about the enormous library – the computer lab to the left, the massive check-out counter in front of it, with the rest of the walls filled with books. On the far side, Mrs. Matt shooed students to the tables next to the periodicals.

"Oh, *whatever,*" Benson said with a groan and entered the Media Center with no idea how much his life was about to change.

Barbie Brigade Pass-Around Notebook
"The Diva Diary"

Monday, Sept. 22nd – Remember, girls, NO NAMES FOR THE SAKE OF PRIVACY!!! I almost got busted with The Diva Diary in math yesterday!! You can even shorten to your birthstone if it's easier! ~ Diamond "Lady Di"

Divas,
    Plan A goes into effect ASAP! Khiara just told everybody in science that Steroid Boy got suspended after this morning's fight, & thank God 4 that! If JH boys want to behave like JH boys, then we'll send them to Exile Island, won't we? N.E. one deviating will be sentenced to a week of niceness to the nerd herd – and u know who they r. Don't let me down, girls. I'm counting on u. ~ Amethyst "Amey"

Divas,
    I'm all about the plan, and nobody's gonna get jack from me, not for a week of nerd herd chatter! Ugh… More 411 – Steroid Boy (we'll refer to him as SB from this point forward) is getting 10 DAYS! Saw him in the office, and not even Aunt Jemima could sweeten him up. Be on your toes – Annika just came into Band and said he's eye-rate! ~ Lady Di

Divas,

Completely eye-rate. His dad just called the office while I was on office runner duty, and man, like father like son. ~ Jade

Divas,

I heard SB isn't coming back...did NE body hear that? Rumor mill's processed the 411 that he told some loser in the office that he's quitting school. Think he can do that? ~ Sapphire "Sapphie"

Paranoid Ones,

Never fear, he won't miss football, not even for sex, right, Amey? And, Sapphie, you need a shorter nickname, I mean, why bother? I just got a "C" on my research paper! How'd the rest of you do? ~ Emerald "Em"

Nosey One,

I have English next hour. Crap – I'm worried now. You spent a whole hour on that paper. I talked to my brother after study hall, and SB is off the team. Coach B. caught wind of the fight and a bunch of other stuff came out. Sources say my brother is out for 2 games. He's pissed royally about that, but rules r rules. He threw a punch and no way around it. No sex talk in here. Everybody's got a price, got it? ~ Amey

Divas,

For my "Sapphie" critics, I looked up my birthstone online during Business and did you know that the ancient Persians believed the earth rested on a giant sapphire and its reflection colored the sky? Yes, so from now on, I will be referred to as Skye (had to add an 'e' or else it would be lame). NEway, it's true – SB's off the team. And I just heard in 2nd hour that his dad's asked for a meeting with the coach and the school board. Yikes. Wouldn't want that man on my bad side. M, is that man as mean as he seems 2 b? ~ Skye

Skye with an e,

Affirmative and + some. ~ Amey

Divas,

Love the new name, Skye with an e. Let's meet at lunch to plan our next step. If Amey's going 4 the HS boys, then the rest of us need to step up 2. We have the names, now let's show those older boys just how precious we are. ~ ◊ (I no longer need a name, I have a symbol…)

◊,

You're a dork, 4 real. ~ Jade

Yeah, are you Prince or something? We'll be there, but I refuse to address you by a symbol. Lady Di might have already been taken, but at least it's royalty! Who would want her name on poker tables around the world being slobbered on by nasty men in wife beater tee shirts with cigars hanging out of their mouths? ~ Skye

Okay, point taken, though some girls might like that opportunity... Of course, none of us, but that goes without saying, right, Divas? ~ Lady Di, the Diva formerly known as ◊

Chapter 8

WHEN THE BELL rang, Benson bolted out of his seat and stuffed his notebooks into his bag. "Hey, Ryan, I'm interviewing Megan in study hall. Guess I should add a little something about my brother's jacket, huh?"

"Wouldn't hurt. Plus, she should want to be real chummy with you now. You're practically related." Ryan let out a laugh as he shouldered his backpack.

Mrs. Matt raised her eyebrows. "Stay professional, Benson. I look forward to reading your assignment." She winked at them as they left, unaware of their flushed faces.

"Wish me luck," Benson said as they headed out of the Media Center, but stopped abruptly when they met a wall of students. In the small commons area between the library and the cafeteria, a mass of Westwood students jumped, stretched, did whatever necessary to see something in the lunchroom. "Man, what's up?"

"I don't know. Maybe Megan knew you were coming and is refusing to let anyone else in," Ryan joked, craning his neck to see. "Crap, c'mon, people, I can't be late for science!"

The hallways leading to their left and back to their right were completely jammed, the cafeteria straight ahead one mass of students pushing each other like cattle.

The throng swayed. Benson tried to keep his feet while being smooshed between bodies. Some-one with a rank case of B.O. made his eyes water. For five or ten seconds, no one moved far enough to get anywhere, overwhelming him with claustrophobia like he'd never experienced. A new wave of kids slammed in behind them, and Benson and Ryan were forty deep and seven students wide with nowhere to go. Benson's equilibrium wavered for a split second, and he had to swallow the panic building in his chest.

He let out a breath as the pack around him loosened slightly. "God, it's not lunch yet. What the heck is going on?" He stretched to see, just able to make out the entryway into the cafeteria. A student ran toward them and another scrambled under a table.

What the hell?

The constant hum of voices around him swallowed any sounds before he could make sense of them.

Is it another fight?

There was a strong push, and the mass of students shuffled backward, a split second before horrific screams curdled Benson's stomach.

"CODE BLUE, I REPEAT, CODE BLUE! TEACHERS – GET STUDENTS TO CLASSROOMS – NOW!" Dr. Jacobsen's voice boomed over the loud speakers. For a few seconds, the pack of teenagers froze.

"I REPEAT, CODE BLUE, WESTWOOD, CODE BLUE!" This time, the tone in Dr. Jacobsen's voice was unmistakable. He sounded frantic, and Benson's heart flew into his throat.

Everybody seemed to shout at once. Ryan screamed at him to do something, but they were wedged in, and students couldn't move on their own. They were like a section on a roller coaster ride, out of control and dependent on the rest of the train.

Another ear-piercing scream hushed the din of noise, and a firecracker popped somewhere in front of them.

This time, the mob took a massive shove backward, and Benson floundered to stay upright. He tried to turn, to twist back toward the Media Center.

Panic shimmered inside him, brimming his eyes with tears. His confusion didn't help.

"That's our intruder drill!" someone screamed in his ear.

The *pop-pop* of more firecrackers sent a sizzle through Benson's insides. *Stop it!* He squeezed his eyes shut trying to unthink what had started clamoring in his head.

"Get back! Everyone, get back!" Mr. Baillargeon, the young ninth grade social studies teacher, shoved kids into the library. "GO! GO! GO!"

Benson, half-twisted, almost fell when a hand grabbed his shirt, got him turned, and tugged him toward the Media Center. Within seconds, Mr. Baillargeon corralled students through the double doors, nearly knocking Benson into the middle frame.

"CODE BLUE! CODE BLUE – NOW!" boomed from the speakers.

Everything felt surreal. The panic of his suspicions and not knowing made his stomach clench tighter. Frantic shouts, the repeated clanking lock bar on the Media Center door – all the chaos roared like a freight train. He had lost Ryan – that scared him more than anything – and in the swarm of people, he couldn't have felt more alone.

"He's bleeding!" a girl shrieked, and that sliver of panic raced down Benson's back right into his privates.

"Far wall, people. Go!" Teachers Benson didn't know barked orders as he was sardined just inside the doorway. Hands grappled with his shirt again and flung him so hard he slammed into the copier against the wall.

Oh my God, oh my God, oh my God. Benson couldn't think. But he knew it was real. He stumbled forward, the possibility racing through his head as they were packed in. *Is it like One Tree Hill last year?* Other scenarios danced on the fringes – bomb threat, escaped convict, some loser robbing the Stop 'n Shop around the corner. They'd gone into lockdown at Field his third grade year when two thugs pulled a bank robbery.

But not this...

He couldn't imagine any of them, but they had been trained for all of it. Lockdown meant there was a direct threat of violence. Not a fire, or they would've been raced outside. No tornadoes in late September, not in Jamestown. Too far from the beach for a hurricane and nowhere near a fault line for an earthquake.

But those beat the heck out of the alternative. Benson's head reeled with all of it. Someone had on way too much cologne, gagging him. He was suddenly aware of body odor again, perfume, someone's breath reeking of vomit. And the screaming that just wouldn't stop. It overloaded his brain and eclipsed his own panic. Claustrophobia seized him, and he elbowed someone as he clamped his hands over his ears, then squeezed his eyes shut.

The sounds piled on top of one another. Screaming teenagers, *and that damn lock bar clacking*. Benson held in his own screams, but bile pressed against his throat, threatening to find its way out. All the crying, babbling about wanting to go home, wanting out, wanting anything but to be trapped here right now with whatever was happening. Benson wanted to shut them all up. SHUT UP!

Bodies pushed against him, pummeling him farther into the library. He couldn't see Ryan, but he needed his best friend, any friendly face at all. Students were pouring in, falling over each other, some talking about all the glass – *what glass?* Another screeched about the blood, that he'd never seen so much blood. Benson tried to unhear, unsee, unthink.

SHUT UP! But he couldn't form words. His brain wouldn't work. The doors finally closed, muffling some of the pande- monium in the hall.

When the doors flew open for another student, a guy yelled, "You're an asshole!" A strange bam-bam-bam followed.

Oh, Jesus, that's gunfire...

Benson spun in search of Ryan. The bedlam renewed, sounding more like a tornado than ever, sweeping through the building, the shouting, the panic, and the smell of terror burning his nose.

He fought his way onto the check-out desk, nearly kicking a girl in the process, but anything was better than being crammed between sweaty bodies. The desk was high enough that just sitting on it allowed him to scan the room. To his right the Media Center doors banged open as the last of the kids streamed in. In front of him and to his left, the library had filled with what seemed like hundreds of students. There was barely any room to walk. With his back to the glass wall that looked into the computer lab and then out into the hallway, he felt vulnerable, but he had to find Ryan.

"Get DOWN, Benson Schmidt, RIGHT NOW!" Mrs. Matt

shouted, and he hopped down, more out of panic than obedience. But he swiveled across the counter and landed on the other side of the counter where there was a little more space. He squatted, like everyone else around him, but stood every few seconds to search for Ryan.

"Inside, now!" Ms. Waters pulled at students jamming in the doorway again. Kids stuck together like Legos, trying to pry themselves free. Every face twisted in panic. Benson peered over heads to watch, recognizing the expressions because they seemed to match the blender in his stomach. Other students climbed over the counter beside him, surrounding him, trapping him, overwhelming him. He continued to bob up and down to scan the room for Ryan.

With the door wedged open in another traffic jam, Benson could hear the total chaos in the hallway that led to the cafeteria. Then a more muffled *pop-pop-pop*, followed by shattering glass.

STOP IT! He clamped his hands over his ears again, but not before another rapid succession of *pop-pop-pop*, closer to the office now. Benson whipped around to look out over the computer lab into the hall. Several kids were sprinting toward the Media Center entrance – or the cafeteria – looking over their shoulders in sheer terror.

No...

"CODE BLUE, WESTWOOD JUNIOR HIGH, CODE BLUE!" The voice of the office secretary, a pitch too high, continued. "WE ARE IN LOCKDOWN, STUDENTS. GET TO THE NEAREST CLASSROOM IMMEDIATELY!"

Benson's head swam. He pushed at students smashing into him – a girl with a pigtail jabbing his neck, a kid shrieking that he'd seen the blood, a lanky boy's elbow pressing into his ear. Claustrophobia consumed him, and Benson closed his eyes again, total panic now stewing his insides. When he thought he might lose it, the pressure of bodies against his chest released, and he almost fell over. He kept his balance by squatting and bracing himself with both hands against the counter. He could see the Media Center doors to his right, the contents of the cabinet in front of him, and crying students to his left.

"Get in the Media Center. Now!" a teacher shouted. Benson could barely hear over the constant shouts and screams of the mob of teenagers. "We're in lockdown! Everyone back as far as you can over there!"

Benson knocked people around to get to his feet, his knees and ankles throbbing, everyone around him in a tornado drill crouch.

God, look at all of them... A sea of kids crammed into the large room – they sensed not to overflow into the computer lab – too accessible from the hallway. Benson ducked his head a little, just thinking about the clear view behind him.

Lockdown. We're really in lockdown... A few more kids scrambled behind the counter and wedged in. At least something separated them from the mass of bodies.

"Lock the damn doors!" Mrs. Matt screamed as she jerked the last of the students through the Media Center doors.

The whole room inhaled. Every conversation stopped. For an instant, there was total silence. Then a girl sniffled, another sobbed, and they heard the sound of someone's feet sprinting down the hallway. Mrs. Mattingly cussing in front of them made it too real. Her blonde hair, usually in a clip or loose around her face, was so mussed, she looked like she had just gotten out of bed.

"No!" Mr. Barker clamored past kids, stepping over some and almost falling. "I just got word that more kids are trying to get here." He held up the Media Center's cordless phone in one hand. He had his cell phone in the other.

Trying? Benson pictured some kid on all fours, crawling down the hall like an army man going for cover.

Three freshmen boys yanked open the Media Center doors, nearly tackled the teachers to get inside, then hid behind the adults like soldiers in battle. At the same instant, the fire alarm screeched to life and hundreds of crying kids clamped hands over their ears. The piercing alarm drowned out the roar of voices, crying, and moaning.

"Boys, over here!" A ninth grade Physics teacher motioned, the man's booming voice able to be heard over the barrage of alarms, sobs, and screams. The teacher was at least six feet six inches tall – several inches taller than Benson's dad – and stood like a lighthouse in the middle of the library, surrounded by kids crouched on the floor. "Can't we lock it now?" the giant man asked Mr. Baillargeon. Other teachers jumped to their feet, as if in solidarity. Benson hadn't realized how many adults were spread throughout the library.

He watched, panicked, as the social studies teacher shook his head no, his chin trembling like he might cry. The maddening squeal of the alarm made his head thud almost more than the stench around him.

"CLEAR THE HALLS, NOW!" screamed Coach Rohart. He opened the door to come in, but turned toward someone in the commons area and took off running in that direction. "HEY!" he yelled as he ran.

Right as the door closed, they heard a girl shriek, "HELP! PLEASE...HELP ME!"

Somebody do something. Benson tried to make sense of it, feeling sick for being grateful it wasn't him out there.

Mr. Baillargeon had been holding the lock bar on one side but let go. Mrs. Matt and Ms. Waters both stayed low and pushed the door open like they meant to help that girl if they could.

No! Don't go...! Benson held his breath, horrified as Mrs. Matt slipped out into the hall. Someone in the middle of the room shouted, "No, Mrs. Matt! Get back here!" But the door closed, eclipsing the blaring alarm that was louder in the hallway. Mrs. Matt shouted something Benson couldn't decipher.

Mr. Baillargeon crouched, then squeezed through the door, motioning for Ms. Waters to stay. The buzzing alarm made it impossible to think. Benson held his hands over his ears again and prayed Mrs. Matt would reappear.

His stomach knotted again. *Get back in here, Mrs. Matt!* Almost instantly, the door yanked open, but it was Mr. Baillargeon who returned and dropped to his haunches. He turned to the mass of students, his face bright red. "Everyone get down! Now! Lock the damn doors!"

Ms. Waters, with trembling hands, inserted a skinny tool

that released the bars on the door. She pushed on both sides to ensure they were locked, then dropped to the floor and put her face in her hands.

Benson wedged a space and sat, not wanting to see or hear anymore. The blaring alarm now filled his head until he couldn't process anything. A ripple of panic swept through the library, and Benson thought he was either going to throw up or wet his pants. Someone had already done both, the stench of urine sour and pungent, vomit rancid, making him dry heave.

The alarms continued to blare, but students fell silent except for the crying. Everyone watched Ms. Waters peering through the narrow windows at something or someone.

Mrs. Matt...

Mr. Baillargeon held the cordless to his ear, plugging a finger in the other. A strange expression spread across his face. Benson thought the teacher might be about to cry.

He dropped his eyes and stared at the items in the cabinet in front of him instead. Reams of paper, ink cartridges, supplies – would these be the last thing he'd see before some maniac came barreling through the doors to kill them all? Right now, anything felt possible.

Flashes of the morning of September 11th made his head throb. Teachers whispering, turning on TVs, and then watching the towers fall while everyone sat stunned in Mrs. Mahoney's room, right in the middle of an art assignment. But he had been so young then. None of it really made sense.

This did.

That's it! Terrorists are bombing Jamestown! It seemed like the most logical thing. Surely no one in Jamestown, or at Westwood, would be capable of anything this horrible.

Students jumped as another rapid series of *pop-pop-pops* echoed down the hall. It sounded like high-powered fire-crackers. Yelps of fear, crying, startled intakes of breath sounded in the crowded room.

"Those're gunshots," a kid in the middle of the room blurted. Benson stared at the guy who had just said what everyone had been thinking. "Someone's pulling a Columbine," another kid muttered.

"Sounded like Black Cat firecrackers to me," another boy argued, but his shaky voice didn't sound too convincing. Random students didn't bother controlling the tears now. Sobbing symphonied in the room like conflicting radio stations.

My God, it's really happened...

"Ah, God! Someone farted! Man, that reeks," a blond-headed boy cried out, followed by gross comments and even nastier smells. Everyone scrambled to get space, to keep from gagging.

In that instant, all alarms shut off, the silence too oppressive. The clocked ticked. Mr. Baillargeon's phone rang. Kids cried. Benson closed his eyes and hummed to fill the void in his brain.

"Hey! Keep your heads down and try to be quiet. We...we don't want them to hear us," Ms. Waters added, then darted her gaze back to the door. Benson couldn't hear everything she said, but he saw with a sick dread that the teachers held hands.

"Hurry!" an adult shouted out in the hall. Scrambling footsteps, then someone screamed, a blood-curdling shriek from horror movies.

"Sit!" Ms. Waters barked at a freshman trying to peek out the small window. Her tone made several younger students yelp. The stench surrounding Benson churned his screwed-up stomach. Farts, sweat, and fresh urine brought a gorge into the base of his throat, and he retched.

A faint whirring made him swallow hard.

Is that a siren? Benson cocked his head, listening. He couldn't tell for sure. He hit the kid next to him on the shoulder. "You hear that?"

Without the alarm, the Media Center was funeral home quiet.

"What?" The kid sat up taller, as if that would help him hear.

"Sirens. I think." *Or maybe I'm going crazy.*

"I..." The boy paused, then added, "Maybe."

Other students beside them nodded, then started whispering. It was either power of suggestion or sheer hope.

After five or six excruciating minutes, doors by the office

banged open, loud shouts and thundering footsteps filled the
hallway. *Police?* There were definite sirens now, much closer
and overlapping. *There are a lot of them!* Benson's heart leapt.
He wanted to stand up and cheer, a clog of emotion filling his
throat. Instead, he held his breath like everyone else in the
Media Center, the tick-tock of the clock like a drumbeat. The
more he tried *not* to hear it, the crazier it made him. Wrapping
his arms around himself, on the brink of completely falling
apart, he prayed silently, something he hadn't done since he
was little.

*I'll do better, God. Please. Get me outta here. I'll tear up
the project. I'll burn my interview notes, I promise.* He let his
breath out slowly and closed his eyes. He tried to pretend he
was somewhere else. Getting plowed by Colin right now would
be okay. Fun even. He'd even eat those lima beans, manure
and all, if it would help.

"Get the hell offa me!" someone in the hall shouted, jerking
Benson back to Westwood Junior High. The entire library
tensed, sensing the climax – sirens whirring outside, people
stomping through the halls, and the teachers' faces finally
hopeful.

The murmuring started as hundreds of kids tried to
speculate about what – and who – had truly happened. Someone blubbered he couldn't believe Jamestown could be one of
them – a Columbine, Paducah, Jonesboro, Red Lake. But
Benson said nothing.

Is that what happened? A Columbine?

His body began trembling, an impending anxiety attack
seizing his chest like a vise. If he didn't get out of the Media
Center soon, he was going to bawl in front of everyone or go
completely mental. That would add to the geekdom he had
attained.

Not that it mattered now.

Ms. Waters' Report

Observation Report
for Westwood Junior High School

Name of witness: _Amy Waters, math teacher_
Date of incident: _Monday, Sept. 22nd_
Time of incident: _passing time before 3rd hour (~9:45)_
Students involved: _Steve Ralston, Michael & Megan Barker (only knowns at this time)_

Description of incident: _(Note to Dr. Jacobsen: Scott Baillargeon is recording the beginning, I am recording the events once in the Media Center.) This Monday I helped supervise students in the wake of a school shooting at Westwood. Approximately 145 students were gathered in the MC following the Code Blue. During that time, Elaine Mattingly, Scott Baillargeon, Travis Spencer, Becky Bennett, Cristine Hayes, and myself were the teachers onsite, plus several aides and student teachers. When the incident started during passing time (around 9:45) I was leaving my supervision in room 116 to go to my classroom downstairs in 024. I heard cracking sounds now known to be gunfire and helped corral kids into the MC. At one point, a young girl cried for help, and Elaine Mattingly left the MC to help. I saw Elaine run into the cafeteria but never saw her return. Scott ran out after her and came back quickly, whispering there was a 'shooter in the lunchroom.' He later told me the boy was Steve Ralston and that Steve had Megan Barker by the throat aiming a pistol at her head. Steve ordered Scott to leave and aimed the gun at him to ensure he did. Scott said he never saw Elaine._

When he came back, we called Mr. Drysdale, were told to

keep the kids as calm as possible, and to wait for the "all clear." It came just after the alarms turned off, and a few minutes later the police arrived. Three officers informed us we needed to log student names, then everyone would be escorted across the street to the First Presbyterian on the corner. Sgt. Mannheim said Dr. Drysdale was calling all the parents (with the help of office staff) and that once kids were marked off the checklist, they could go home. He would NOT allow students to leave with parents who were in the circle drive or parking lot. They were told to come to the church and wait for their children to be cleared so we could make sure all kids were accounted for.

After creating the chart and going over all the names using the office's roster, it was determined that sixteen students and four adults were unaccounted for. For sake of record, those people are:

Adults: Coach James Rohart, Elaine Mattingly, Sarah Connors, and Frank Vernon.

Students: Evan Anderson, Megan Barker, Michael Barker, Malakai Jeffries, Tyler Leslie, Tasha Mountjoy, Steve Ralston, Reed Robinson, Jennifer Slakhaur, Tim Silvey, Graham Stevonovich, Jerius Taylor, Alex Thackeray, Ty Willingham, Lawrence Wyatt, and Kevin Young. Mr. Baillargeon, Mr. Spencer and I waited until 4:30 at which time all parents had been reached and every student picked up. Note: Overheard several snips of conversation between students, so it seemed appropriate to add it here so you have access to all pertinent information. According to Pam Utterbeck, Steve Ralston was in the office waiting for his parents to come get him because he'd gotten suspended for a fight in the cafeteria before school this morning (he was already serving ISD for a similar incident). He was furious, she said, ranting about how he would not let this go, that she would be punished, and his buddies had screwed up big time. She said she asked who "she" was, but he just stared at her. She watched him scrawl names in ink on his jeans, confused that they were all football players, even one high school guy. She gave me those names: Ty, Michael, Malakai, Alex, Reed,

Evan, Jerius, and Colin. He rambled on about cheerleaders thinking they're all that, and Jenni had blabbed her fat mouth for the last time. Fuming that his so-called teammates and friends wouldn't turn their backs on him ever again, he bragged to Pam that he'd teach them a lesson. When Megan Barker walked into the office to report for her office runner duties, Pam said he went ballistic because she had on a letter jacket, apparently the cause of the fight before school. Steve told her to take it off, and Megan told him to f-off. Steve ran out of the office shouting, "Bitch!" Randy McCracken was also in the office waiting to go home because he was ill, she said, so he should be able to corroborate her statement. None was said loud enough for the secretaries to hear except the last word Steve shouted as he left.

Benson's Journal

Monday, September 22nd

    I don't even know how to talk about today, but after being smothered by Mom and Dad for the past three hours, I have to vent.

    All the crying, holding me and saying how scared they were...would they have been different if it had been Colin?

    I don't know. Makes me feel like crap just thinking it. Ryan called. We talked for a long time. He's going to try to come over when his mom's Valium and his dad's scotch kick in. Poor guy...I think my life's hard. Can't imagine being an only child, especially after today.

    When the police came in, these three officers escorted us to the circle drive right past the office. There was all this broken glass and bullet holes in the wall. It freaked me out. We had to cross the street to First Presbyterian Church, and if our parents were there, they checked us off a list and let us go. Ryan's mom was wailing at the top of her lungs when she saw him. Seeing my mom cry – which I don't think I've EVER seen, it did funky things to me - I bawled like a baby. And so did practically every other kid who came out. It was like pulling a plug or something. Ms. Waters was a mess. I asked her about you, but she said she didn't know anything. From the terrible look on her face, I think she was lying, and that made my stomach hurt. I just can't stand not knowing. I feel like I'm writing to you, but I don't know if you're okay. It feels weird. You weren't there when we got outside. There was SWAT and these other task forces and stuff. And we saw tons of teachers, except you.

Sorry about that. Had to get a soda and couldn't see too good to write anyway. I mean, this whole journal is for you, Mrs. Matt. I just wish someone would've told us something, anything. But it was weird how none of us really got any details.

When we got in the car, Dad got all ticked about the whole thing, saying some lowlife with a gun could sure give a good school a bad name. Then he took me to McDonald's – I probably could've asked for a new car today and gotten it – and even though I didn't feel much like eating, I got my usual Double Quarter Pounder with cheese meal deal. I didn't eat much of it, but I think it made them feel better to feed me.

Right after the radio said there would be no school tomorrow, Dad asked what I saw. Mom shushed him, telling him it wasn't "appropriate," but I gave him a short version anyway. Tried to find out what they heard, and Dad shared a little about what the radio was saying. Nothing that we didn't really already have figured out except they released that the shooter had been arrested. Made Mom mad at him, but it doesn't take much lately. She's been prosecuting a huge case, and I feel guilty

*that she had to leave court just 'cause of me. Dad
didn't say where he was. He's a chemical engineer
and travels all the time. It sounded like maybe he
was heading to the airport for a meeting in Dallas.*

*When I went downstairs for a soda, both of them
were working on their laptops but jumped up when
I came into the kitchen. Mom offered to make me
something, but I reminded her I had McDonald's.
Do you think she forgot? Dad said he'd shoot hoops
or kick the ball around with me. But we've never
EVER kicked a ball around together. I don't think
he knows what else he and I would do together. He
and Colin would shoot hoops or play catch. I really
just wish they'd go back to work.*

*You know what's sad, Mrs. Matt? I don't think
they can relate to the 'School Benson' at all. I mean,
Mom was a homecoming queen, president of her
class, and Dad was captain of every sport he
played. I think both even got named most likely to
succeed, and they went to big schools somewhere in
San Diego. When Colin was born, we moved out
here, a thousand miles from their relatives and
close to D.C., since that's where Mom's hoping to
end up some day. She wants to be a big-city
prosecutor or even a Supreme Court judge. No
matter how crummy last week was for Ryan and
me, their merry little world just kept right on
spinning. So how can they even imagine what my
life is like? Or the crap we've gotten ourselves in the
middle of?*

*Oh, God... Mrs. Matt, you don't think something
we did might've caused this, do you? I'm going to*

listen to the radio and then get on the Internet and see what I can find out. If anything Ryan and I did caused this, I could never live with myself.

Ryan's Journal

Monday, September 22nd

Mom and Dad are certifiable. I wish my parents were like Benson's...equals and both big-wig business people. Mom is like this perfect little doctor's wife, cleaning and cooking, but then when life throws a curve ball, she falls apart. Dad had to give her a sedative. I wonder what she would do if she hadn't married a cardiologist? I guess he wasn't one when she married him. But you get the point. She sure takes a lot of pills for someone who doesn't even work. So it won't be long before she's zonked and I can skate over to Benson's. It's a long walk, but there's not a prayer Dad will take me. At the rate he's downing the scotch, he's not far behind Mom.

Mrs. Matt, this kind of stuff doesn't make any sense. Why would someone bring a gun to school and shoot anybody? What's that going to solve except send you to jail or a grave? How can a sane person want that?

I just don't get it. I wish you had been out there when they sent us home. You would've told us stuff. I think I'll call Tim and see what he knows. If anyone can get the scoop, it's him.

Okay, no one's home at Tim's – that's weird. I'm going to call Pam next, but I've come to one conclusion... I should've never taken my peace stickers off the lunchroom table or my closet or my binders. I lost my focus. We started Operation Cappuccino to get rid of all the crap. But it doesn't matter, not with all the stupid violence in the world. I should've known better.

I sort of remember Columbine on TV, or maybe it was the anniversaries I've seen. Anyway, it just makes me sick that our school is going to be famous for something like this. Last year, everyone buzzed about that episode of One Tree Hill...some even said that crap would never happen here.

Shows how much they know.

Chapter 9

"LISTEN TO THIS," Ryan said, as he barreled into Benson's bedroom, not bothering with hello.

"Hello to you, too." Benson hit mute on the TV, disgusted by the reporters outside his school blabbing about how they never dreamed this would happen in Jamestown. *Who ever thinks it's going to happen to them?*

"You gotta hear what Pam said." Ryan grabbed Benson's McDonald's cup, drained the rest of the soda, then burped.

"You're welcome," Benson snipped, then added, "So you've been on the phone." Having been in a funk, he couldn't imagine calling people and rehashing the whole thing – not yet. The image of Mrs. Matt dashing out the Media Center doors wouldn't go away.

"We have to go to Memorial Hospital. That's where everyone is. Tim's one of them."

"What?" Benson's stomach clamped, already gurgling around what little of the Quarter Pounder and fries he'd eaten.

"He and at least seven other students have been admitted. Some are in surgery, it sounds like. You're not listening to the radio? No one's saying what teachers got hurt. Coach Rohart supposedly got shot. No word yet on Mrs. Matt. I've called everyone I could think of."

"Man, Mom and Dad aren't going to let me go. No way." Benson thought about it for a minute, hating for the millionth time that he didn't have the independence of a driver's license. "Who are the other students? Do you know?"

"Huh-uh. They're not releasing names. But at least ten kids are, you know..." Ryan's voice tapered, dropping into the chair at Benson's desk. It took him a few minutes to continue, both of them weighing the reality of ten classmates dying, and the possibility that they might have known any of them. "Pam says one adult was killed. Her mom heard it on the police scanner. And they're all at Memorial. We really gotta get over there, Benson. I mean, Tim, he's our friend."

"How're we going to get there?" Benson sat on the edge of his bed, wishing he could get the swirling sensation out of his stomach. "Is Pam going?"

"Yeah, her parents were taking her. Randy's already there. She said he saw Steve come to school this morning looking like he hadn't slept or showered. After the cafeteria fight before school, Steve got suspended. Pam said Steve was in the office when Megan came in to do her office runner thing, and get this." Ryan paused.

Benson didn't say a thing. His stewing insides wouldn't let him. He waited for Ryan to continue as he stared at the silent television screen, ignoring the same images of the outside of Westwood.

"She still had on Colin's letter jacket, and Steve freaked out, right in front of Pam and the secretaries. Completely lost it, shouting at her. Pam said he yanked open the office door, kicked stuff, even called Megan a bitch as he left. She said he was totally out of it, eyes glazed like he was high. She thinks he must've run all the way home and gotten his hands on a gun."

"A nine-millimeter, no less."

"How do you know that?" Ryan sounded impressed.

"Dad heard it on the radio. I've been watching for more news and listening to KJTL, but they just keep saying the same crap. I was sure Tim would call. Now I know why he didn't." He shook his head and ran a hand through his sweaty hair. He felt grimy on the inside and out. "Think we could call the hospital and check on him?"

"My dad already did. Talked to Mr. Silvey, and it sounded like Tim is going to be okay. At least that's what Dad said. The Silveys weren't like postal or anything. Several people said they tried to call you, but got the mom block, so they all called me. I told them a little about *Operation Cappuccino*. Not anything major, just the concept. Hope you don't care."

"No point guarding our stories now. Except I don't really want teachers or Dr. Jacobsen finding out about it. What else

did you hear about Megan? Jesus, I wonder if Colin knows."
Benson bowed his head, an odd sense of camaraderie washing
over him, but it slipped away before he could dwell on it.

"Pam told me Steve had been scrawling names on his
jeans, and Colin's was one of them. I heard high school
practice was cancelled and they let out early, too. I think they
got out at 1:15."

Benson looked at his clock. 2:45. His world had been
rocked only a few hours earlier, but it seemed like days ago.
What would he say when Colin got home? He wanted to hate
Colin for invading his world, but it seemed stupid now.

Benson sprawled across the bed on his stomach, chin
resting on forearms, flipping through channels. "I can't stand
being trapped here. We don't even know who's hurt."

"Randy was in the office getting ready to go home sick.
Apparently he had an Algebra test he wasn't ready for. He's just
sitting there when all of a sudden on the secretary's walkie-
talkie someone screams that three students had just been shot,
to get an administrator and call 911. Within three minutes, he
said, all hell broke loose. And when they screamed there was
shooting in the cafeteria, everyone was crammed into the back
part of the office, behind desks and stuff. He said it was like
forever, then some freshman football player came barreling in,
pulling a cheerleader by the hair, screaming and waving a pistol.
Said he looked wilder than that guy in *Natural Born Killers*."

"You mean to tell me that Randy doesn't know who Steve
Ralston is?"

"I guess not. I asked him several times. I even asked if the
girl was Megan. Randy just said they all looked alike to him."

Benson laughed at the irony and then immediately felt
guilty for it.

"He did say that when one of the secretaries, Mrs. Connors,
tried to talk to the guy, he shot her in the stomach without
batting an eye."

"Damn." Benson tried to picture it, but it was just too
bizarre. They sat for several long minutes, not much left to be
said. Benson didn't like the scene that kept playing out in his
head.

"I'm going to get a soda. Your parents aren't going to be weirded out if I go down there, are they?"

"Naw, bring me one too. And if they offer you cookies, be polite and take one. Mom's cracked out the rolled dough like she thinks being domestic is going to help me. Parents are strange."

"What kind?"

"Probably chocolate chip. Me and Colin make 'em every now and then, but I've never seen Mom do it. Might be edible. Who knows?" Benson flopped back on his bed as Ryan headed down the hall toward the stairs. The sound of his footsteps catapulted Benson's head back to Westwood hours earlier.

I wonder what Megan thought when she saw Steve coming at her with a gun...

His brain couldn't wrap around the absurdity of it. He closed his eyes, trying to imagine what it would feel like to have a gun rammed into his temple, the comfort of house sounds lulling him. *If I think about something else, maybe I can make it all go away.*

Seconds later, he drifted to sleep.

Benson's Dream

THE EDGES WERE fuzzy, and Benson understood the movie in his head wasn't real.

But knowing it didn't stop his brain from shutting down from exhaustion. He wandered aimlessly through Jamestown's downtown district, not sure why he was there or even how he got there. He trekked up Broadway, glancing in the windows of shops he'd grown up seeing. The shoe store his mom loved, the pet shop where he kept seeing puppies he wanted...

The distant sound of cheering drifted toward him. An announcer boomed, "Oh, man, that was CLOSE!"

He looked down Broadway as he crossed 44th Street. The sidewalks were packed as usual with mid-day shoppers, so he couldn't see too far.

A band erupted into the touchdown song, followed by people shouting "We're gonna kick the hell outta you...you... you, you, you!" And the song repeated, accompanied by the clear rhythm of cheerleaders, though he couldn't decipher the cheer.

In downtown Jamestown?

"Oooh, inches!" the same booming voice cried. The crowd gasped, the sharp collective intake unmistakable. Where is that?

Benson hurried down Broadway, past 45th Street, then broke into a jog toward 46h.

"Folks, this could get ugly!" the announcer shouted, and the stands erupted with "U-g-l-y, you ain't got no alibi..." The chant continued as Benson sped up, almost sprinting.

The crowd noise grew louder, the band launched into "Hey, Baby," and everyone sang, igniting the festive fervor.

"That Mustang's gonna make it interesting!" the announcer called out, and the crowd groaned.

Benson raced toward 47th and Broadway, suddenly blocked by a wall of people. A mob lined both sides of the streets, staring at something in the middle. He couldn't see over them, couldn't see the street or the intersection, couldn't figure out what kind of game this was or who was playing.

The announcer cried, "You can sure handle that spotlight, kid!"

Benson cringed...that was something people told his brother all the time, and Colin taunted Benson with it.

'You can't handle the spotlight, can you, Wimp Breath?'

By third grade, Colin's shadow spread bigger and darker over him. Even if he didn't like it there, it was safe in the decaying fungus of Colin's damp underworld.

"That Mustang's on a mission!" the announcer said. "You better brace yourself, kid! Your brother ain't savin' ya!"

Benson grimaced, certain the voice meant him. He shoved his way through the crowd, fifteen to twenty people deep. Many of them chanted Go... go...go...go...

The rhythm of their cries made his stomach seize in panic...who? What?

Benson shuddered.

"Always a spectator," the announcer hissed. "Never the hero."

Benson fought his way to the curb, frantic to understand what the sudden steady clapping was for. A mass of people stared first at the intersection, then down Broadway at something. He followed the eyes of the gawking crowd.

"Oh, my God..." He recognized the kitchen chair sitting in the dead center of the 47th and Broadway intersection.

Colin sat patiently in it as if waiting for a seven-course meal, just lounging as rush hour traffic whipped past him so fast the sleeves of his shirt slapped against his arms. His brother's face basked in the sun, upturned as if praying. His blond hair blew away from his face, longer than normal – than now – but it wasn't the hair that was wrong. Perfect features accented pale blue eyes that squinted into a gorgeous afternoon sky – not giving traffic a single glance.

A Cadillac Escalade roared inches from his right shoulder,

the announcer shouting, "Another close one. Man, that kid's got a set!"

"No!" Benson screamed. "Get up, Colin!" But the sound died in his throat. His feet, frozen to the curb, simply would not budge.

He stared at the traffic light, waited for it to go yellow. And continued to wait. Ten seconds... another agonizing five. The stoplight refused to cooperate.

"Here it comes!" the announcer boomed, and everyone around Benson answered with a hearty Yes! The clapping grew louder, steady and well-paced.

Screeching tires jerked Benson's attention to the street a few blocks down. A sleek black Mustang two hundred yards away weaved through intersections, zooming in and out of traffic like a fugitive. It was headed straight for his brother like a wolf tracking a rabbit.

"Get up! Colin!"

His brother turned toward him, and Benson shivered.

"Always a spectator," Colin whispered.

How could Benson hear that over the roar of cars and all the people?

He watched the Mustang, then looked frantically back at Colin, a zing of panic ripping him open from the inside out.

It dawned on Benson that Colin wasn't strapped to the chair or tied down, nothing holding him there. He was just sitting and waiting. For what? Did he want to die?

Why would someone with an absolutely perfect life want to kill himself?

The Mustang's tires squealed with every assertive jerk, and Benson volleyed his glance from the Ford to his brother and back.

He felt like a spectator at a cruel tennis match.

The Mustang bared its teeth and closed the gap between it and Colin.

"Always a spectator..."

Benson tried to move...he didn't want to be a spectator anymore. But his Reeboks had melted to the concrete. The sports car's engine growled, mocking him as it raced through the last intersection before reaching Colin's. There his brother sat, right in the middle of the 47th and Broadway stoplight.

"GO!" the green light demanded.

Benson's heart accelerated with each rev of the Mustang's engine. Colin met the eyes of the car's headlights. Time slowed like the flow of cooling lava. Benson's world swam out of focus.

"NO!" He screamed as loud as he could, yet his voice evaporated inches from his face as the wind swirled around him.

Metal suddenly crunched metal. Cars that never slowed were plowed by the kamikaze Mustang, instant junkyard scrap. The force drove the mangled mess into the intersection, and amidst the glass, chrome, steel, and Benson's screams, pieces of handcrafted oak sprayed high into the sky. Out of nowhere, a football came hurtling through the air.

Colin dove. His outstretched fingers caressed the ball like a mother holding her baby, and brought it in for a phenomenal catch. A nano-second later, the Mustang plowed into him, severing his neck from his body.

Colin never released the football. The section of the car's hood that sliced through his throat was splattered with blood. The Mustang coughed and sputtered before it died for good.

Benson dropped to his knees, ignoring the jolting pain that shocked his spinal chord. Concrete chewed both knee-caps. He went down on all fours, the wind knocked out of him, his spirit keening with the knowledge of what he'd just seen. He heaved like a retching dog.

Tears streaked his dirty cheeks. The irony of the catch was not lost on Benson.

A loudspeaker in his mind boomed, "WOW! What a catch by Schmidt! What a heads-up play! Number 28 comes through in a clincher. Holy cow, that kid is amazing!"

Hysterical giggles swelled in Benson's chest as he thought to clarify that there was no head on number 28 anymore. He thought he was going to explode and could no longer suppress it.

Howls of laughter erupted from him, immediately inter-laced with tears of shock and loss.

When he thought the tears would never stop, someone shook him, jerked him awake.

Chapter 10

"BENNIE! HEY! WHAT the..."

Benson bolted upright and wiped the spittle from his mouth. "Oh, God, I must've fallen asleep." He glanced over at the clock on his desk, his clothes rumpled from writhing on his bed in the midst of the strange dream. A whopping ten minutes – *felt like days* – but the vapor of it still clung to him.

"You were laughing like a maniac. That musta been some dream." Ryan took a sip of Dr Pepper and offered him a cookie, staring hard into his blurry eyes. "You okay, man?"

He nodded, trying to ease his jangling nerves.

Residue from the dream flitted away, the weird game of chicken between Colin and a Mustang. Not sure what to make of it, he didn't say anything as he took a cookie, his hands still trembling. After several minutes of deep breaths, the world began righting itself.

How do I explain that one to Ryan? He may think I've totally crunched my chips.

"Hey, look!" Ryan shouted, before Benson had to make a decision.

Ryan grabbed the remote and hit the volume until the speakers of the tiny Magnavox rattled.

"...we bring you this special announcement," a voice said, as a still shot of Westwood Junior High filled the screen.

"The barrage of school shootings has come to our quiet Jamestown community," a young reporter announced, like she was trying for her own George Polk Award. She talked while walking toward the circle drive. "It was a grisly scene this afternoon at Westwood Junior High. A ninth grade boy entered school with a nine-millimeter and opened fire on classmates, adults, and took an eighth-grader hostage. Ten are confirmed dead, two adults in critical condition, and numerous students are being treated for injuries. It is unconfirmed at this time whether the hostage was one of the injured or not. As a community, we cannot comprehend such a senseless act of violence occurring in Jamestown. There will be a candlelight vigil here tonight at sundown..." She waved her hand dramatically toward the sign in front of Westwood that claimed it was one of the nation's finest schools.

Not anymore.

Her voice droned on as video of Westwood Junior High hallways goose pimpled Benson's arms and legs. Finally some real news about the shooting, but seeing it for real brought back the claustrophobia from the media center. The camera zoomed in on shell casings littering the hallway, then zipped past what Benson thought might be blood splatter on the cafeteria floor.

Just like they had speculated, the whole shooting took place between the cafeteria, down the hall past the Media Center, and into the main office. It was a miracle more students hadn't gotten shot.

Always a spectator slithered through his brain. A remnant from the dream? *But I'm doing something now, aren't I?*

"That's the crap Mrs. Matt was talking about. It's why we started this project, to be real journalists, right?" Benson trembled, partly from the sight of the Media Center, but mostly thinking about the possibility that his favorite teacher might be one of the victims.

The camera panned to papers strewn about the office and toppled chairs, but pulled back, careful not to show too much. *Why stop now?* Dr. Jacobsen's office door, centered on the screen, was blurred as numbers appeared on the screen for anyone who might need counseling, want more information about the aftermath of school shootings, and a suicide hotline.

Had it been Megan with Steve in that office? Was she the one he dragged down the hall? A sudden chill made Benson shudder.

The reporter spoke softly as images of a taped football practice played. "The shooter has been described as a star athlete and strong student," she explained, the camera breaking from the practice to zoom in on the championship banners hanging in the gym. She continued, but Benson lowered the volume enough to hear the TV and be able to talk too.

"It's gotta be Ralston. All they see is the jock, and they actually glorify him as an athlete." He grunted in disgust. "Even after this."

"Strong student, my ass. With the help of some cheat sheets maybe." Ryan humphed. "And a little extortion."

"That's some scary shit, ain't it?" a voice behind them said.

Benson whirled to see Colin standing in the doorway, a strange expression on the older boy's face. Not the usual cocky demeanor – his brother's normally tucked-in shirt hung half out, and his cheeks had rosy splotches that met dark circles under bloodshot eyes.

Benson's head swam for an instant, images from his dream overlapping with Colin being here now. *No kitchen chair or Mustang bearing down on you…I don't think.* "You look like crap."

"Weird day, huh?" Ryan turned the TV almost all the way down as Colin came in and plopped on the edge of the bed.

That last catch was a doozy – you seem to have your head back. Another surge of laughter built in Benson's chest, totally out of place. He felt off-kilter for second or two, almost dizzy. The dream kept interfering and replacing what he'd just seen on TV, both too bizarre to be real.

"Yeah. How 'bout you guys? You okay?" Colin asked, an odd look of concern on his face. Benson had never seen it before, and for a fleeting moment wondered why some brothers were the best of friends and others fought like rival gang-bangers.

"Yeah, I guess." Benson honestly didn't know what he felt, but a sudden wave of anger surged through him. *Your damn jacket nearly got all of us killed, Colin!*

But he said nothing. The jacket hadn't gotten the ball rolling; his interview had. Hadn't it? So many times Colin ticked him off for no reason at all, but Benson was too tired to be pissed. Too tired and too unsure of his own role in the day's events.

"Guess you heard about my jacket," Colin mumbled, his voice barely a whisper. He stared at the TV as they continued to show shots of Westwood. Benson watched his brother, not knowing what to say, shocked that Colin had read his mind.

"We heard," Ryan finally said. "No practice today, huh?"

"Got cancelled since school let out early. Coach wasn't thrilled, but who could think about football today?"

Benson cringed. *I did in my dream, I guess.* But on a deeper level, he understood that dream had nothing to do with football.

"You guys see anything?" Colin asked without looking up at them.

Benson narrowed his eyes. *Is that why you're here? On a fishing expedition?* Colin seldom stepped foot in Benson's room except to accuse him of a crime – swiping money or peeking at the magazines under his brother's mattress.

"We got shoved into the Media Center. Something was going down in the cafeteria while we were right in the commons area, and..." Benson's voice hitched, caught on the realization that he had been mere feet from possible death. He let out a long sigh and looked to Ryan for help. His red-headed friend's pained expression mirrored his.

"From what we've figured out, Steve Ralston had Megan in the cafeteria, shot a bunch of people, and then dragged her to the office." Ryan hesitated, crinkling his forehead. "Why do you think he did that? I mean, why the office?"

"Maybe he was pissed at the principal for suspending him," Benson suggested. But that didn't make sense. Why *did* Ralston bother going to the office? If he meant to kill Megan, why not just do it in the cafeteria and make a run for it?

"He wanted answers, and then probably tried to reason with her. You know, convince her with a Glock that he was the right man for her." Colin gave an odd chuckle. Benson had never seen such contempt on his brother's face. "He's a control freak. And he probably thought staring down the barrel of a gun would help her realize breaking up with him was a mistake."

"Jesus," Benson mumbled. "Like that would work?"

"How'd she get your jacket, Colin?"

Pow! Ryan laid it on the table. Benson sucked in air, caught off guard by his best friend's guts and envious he didn't have the same kahunas.

"I must've left it at the party Saturday night. Maybe she used it to make Ralston jealous. I don't know. But that dude's been getting juiced since last winter. Rumor has it he wanted to play varsity ball this year. Thought if he bulked up, the coaches couldn't ignore him. But the only guys who ever move up are quarterbacks, receivers, and running backs."

"So, I don't get it. She was breaking up with Steve because he was on steroids and went out with you instead?" Benson hadn't meant to say it out loud, didn't want to start anything that might stoke Colin to take pent-up aggressions out on him.

"We didn't go out," Colin countered, a look of denial that didn't ring too true. "I talked to her a little bit, but this party wasn't for kids. She and a bunch of her rah-rah group crashed it. None of my friends would ever invite Nikki Harmon to anything. That chick's off the charts."

Off the charts? What's that mean? Benson peeked at Ryan, and he could tell his best friend was on the same wavelength. *We thought all preps liked each other, just by association.*

"So you left your jacket at a party and didn't go back looking for it? I've never seen you without that jacket. Ever." Benson crossed his bedroom and went into the adjoining bathroom to pee. He pushed the door mostly closed, but listened. If Colin wanted to add anything, he would tell Ryan quicker than he would tell his little brother.

"Me and Megan weren't going out. Why would you guys think that?"

"The Barbie Brigade said she had a new high school boy-friend. Benson overheard them. So when she showed up in your jacket, we just assumed. Plus, Pam Utterbeck heard that you two were pretty chummy at the party." Ryan's tone amazed Benson – no fear, no worry about a beat-down. That would come later for Benson if Colin felt compelled.

"The Barbie Brigade is full of crap, and so is Pam. I might have talked to Megan a little, but that's it. I hate the damn gossip. And what those bimbos *don't* know is that a bunch of crap happened last weekend when Ralston and a few of his buddies came to a party after our game. It's a long story, but bottom line is that Ralston was on the edge. Now he's screwed up royally, and I'm glad. She can finally have some peace." Colin ran both hands across his face, then through his short blond hair.

Benson emerged from the bathroom, trying to send brain-waves to Ryan, who was already furrowing his brow. *If he barely knows her, why does he care? Besides, doesn't he realize she's probably been shot?*

"He shot a bunch of people today, Colin," Ryan said, clearly trying to help him make the connection. "Even shot a couple of teachers and a secretary."

Benson couldn't stop staring at his brother's stricken face. They sat in silence for a few minutes, Benson mulling over what Colin had said. He took a deep breath, mustering the courage to ask the question he most wanted to know.

"You think she's the one he took to the office?" Benson looked at the TV, avoiding his brother's eyes. When nobody said anything – and he knew Ryan wouldn't because they had already speculated that it had been Megan – he finally looked up.

His bladder seized at Colin's blanched face. His brother stood, shook his head like he was having a conversation with himself, then lunged into the bathroom and puked. The two younger boys stared at each other, but Benson didn't know what to think. Colin came back into the room, swaying like an unsteady foal.

"You okay?" Ryan jumped up and offered to help, but Colin waved a hand like he didn't need anything and dropped onto the bed.

What gives? Benson felt queasy, like an intruder as he watched his brother. Colin the Rock's vulnerability evoked an odd emotion in Benson – sympathy maybe?

He marched into the bathroom and poured Colin a glass of water, then wetted a washcloth. Never one to play caretaker, Benson just couldn't ignore his brother's pain.

Wow...things sure have a way of turning upside down and inside out.

Acknowledging that something about the shooting had changed him, he grappled with his altered outlook on life. On the future. *Maybe Operation Cappuccino opened my eyes, too.*

"So you think Megan got shot? Is that it?" Muscles twitched in Colin's face, his eyes red, but if tears threatened, Benson couldn't see them.

"That would make the most sense," Ryan said. Colin stared at the floor. Benson stared at his brother. "She supposedly broke up with Steve like weeks ago, at the end of the summer or something. But he kept coming around. So Michael popped Steve a good one in the mouth and told him to stay the hell away from Megan. And now Steve comes to school packing heat. I mean, with all the crap he's been dishing, who else would he take into that office?"

Benson made eye contact with Ryan – *I'm the one who passed along Steve's words of wisdom that fueled those fires. Not much of a spectator in that game.*

He squeezed his eyes shut and waited for the blob in his throat to either balloon or pass. *Mrs. Matt is really going to kick my ass when she finds out.* A feeble *if* drifted through his head, but he refused to acknowledge it. Mrs. Matt had to be okay. He wouldn't accept any alternatives

"We've gotta find out," Colin insisted, his face brightening at the prospect of answers. Either that or he was on the verge of a total meltdown.

"I have an idea," Ryan suggested. "Let's call Megan's house. If she's okay, she'll be home, right?"

Benson cringed. *How cold if she isn't...* But it made sense if Colin really wanted to know. They didn't even have to give their names.

"Yeah! Let's do it." Colin jumped up, grabbing Benson's cordless phone and handing it to Ryan. *Like we're all just the best of buddies.*

But an odd feeling settled in Benson's gut. He liked being treated like a person by his brother, not a punching bag.

"What's her number?" Ryan held it ready to dial, but didn't seem too thrilled about it.

"Uh, twenty-seven forty. 555-2740." Colin rubbed his hands together.

Benson furrowed his brow, then side-glanced Ryan, who punched the numbers into the phone. Their eyes met, and the wavelength was clear.

If he just met her Saturday, how's he know her number by heart already?

Chapter 11

RYAN THREW THE phone at Colin in a panic. "It's ringing!" He acted shocked that it had the nerve.

Colin's quick hands grabbed the handset and pressed it to his ear just in time to ask for Megan.

Benson held his breath, waiting, watching. Colin suddenly squeezed his eyes shut.

Uh-oh.

His brother's hands trembled. "Uh, wh...where is she?" He screwed up his face in a bellyache expression Benson hadn't seen since Colin's bout of flu two years ago.

He's gonna cry, or puke again. Benson bowed his head, remembering a time when he and Colin crashed their bikes headlong into the massive stone at the corner of Mulberry and Addison. Both boys fisted away the tears, trying to maintain their macho demeanor. He had been six, Colin ten. That was the last time he could ever remember seeing his brother cry. Even when he sprained an ankle or got his eyelid cut during a football game in Mighty Mights.

"I understand. Um, ma'am, do you know if she can have visitors?" Colin raked a hand over his closely cropped dish-water hair and took a deep breath without letting it out right away. A tear slipped down his cheek.

Visitors. Benson grimaced.

"It must've been her," Ryan whispered.

Benson felt a strange surge of empathy for his brother, and a flash of memory startled him. *I took a nasty fall off my bike, and Colin raced to my rescue. I was like 3 or 4.* Benson remembered Colin, who was still a god to him then, had practically carried him home. And it was Colin who cleaned the cuts while his mom put bandages all over his legs.

"Can any of us see her?"

The long pause made everything more surreal – remembering being little, watching his older brother now so vulnerable, but mostly, Benson worried about Mrs. Matt. Just being part of it had severed something inside of him. *Operation Cappuccino* didn't seem all that important anymore.

"Yes, ma'am." Colin nodded.

I don't wanna ever go back to that place. I'll make Mom and Dad take me to another school. Just the idea of going into the Westwood Media Center sent shudders through him. And that his brother was talking to someone at the Barker's house about their daughter – their *wounded* daughter – made it even stranger.

"Okay, but will they let in people who aren't family?" Colin squeezed his eyes shut again, listening.

Benson didn't know how to describe how disconnected he felt. He wanted to cry, yet he didn't want to breathe. *Is it just me?* He stared at Ryan, whose eyes were wide with worry. *Maybe not.*

Colin started rustling through the mess on Benson's desk. "Yeah, hang on. Let me get a pen." He rummaged until he found one, then ripped the McDonald's receipt off the bag. He scribbled something on it. "Thank you so much." Colin hung up, then let out a long sigh.

"Well?" Benson was afraid Colin would dash out of the bedroom and not tell them anything. He couldn't handle any more *not knowing.* For a second, it didn't seem like Colin could talk.

"Megan's at Hamilton Memorial in ICU," Colin finally blurted. Letting out little bursts of air, like he was warming up for a race, he added, "Her prognosis isn't good. Those were Ramona's exact words. She's the housekeeper and had just happened to stop by the house to drop off Megan's school stuff and get things for the family to stay overnight."

Benson raised his eyebrows. "And? Are you going to get to see her?"

"Not yet, but friends are in the waiting room. Sounds like tons of people are there because of other students and some teachers. Coach Rohart and Mrs. Matt are both in ICU too. I'm, um, I'm...going."

Mrs. Matt... Benson lost air, like he'd been punched in the gut. His heart skipped, then fluttered like it might stop beating. *Someone yelled, 'Help me,' and she didn't even hesitate. Who's gonna save you, Mrs. Matt?*

Colin headed toward the hall, then stalled in the doorway looking back at them. "You guys comin'?"

Benson's mouth fell open. *He's inviting us to go with him?* But his legs wouldn't cooperate. Ryan mumbled something about their project, how Mrs. Matt had to be okay so she could see what an awesome job they'd done. On the silent TV screen, the same reporter stood outside Westwood Junior High probably saying the same things over and over. *Leave us alone...*

"I'm not waiting forever. C'mon." Colin marched into his own bedroom, rattled keys, and then paused in the hallway.

Benson elbowed Ryan, ESP for, *You believe this?* Both headed out after Colin, following the sophomore who had never invited them to go anywhere for anything unless it involved a bribe.

Maybe we'll finally know what really happened, and Mrs. Matt will wake up and tell us that Operation Cappuccino didn't push Steve Ralston over the edge.

Benson nearly ran to catch up, Ryan right with him. Even if it was an ulterior motive for Colin, at least it felt like they were doing something proactive.

He rarely rode in his brother's prized Mazda unless he overslept or their parents ordered Colin to take Benson somewhere. And every time, Colin griped about having a snot-nosed kid brother and being a "damn taxi service."

"What about Mom and Dad? And Ryan's folks?" Benson asked. "They're not gonna let us go. They're too worried about us."

"Leave that up to me," Colin said, tramping downstairs without another word.

"What the heck is he gonna say?" Ryan glanced at his watch. "I'll have to call Dad."

"He's got a screw loose." The two boys tiptoed to the top of the stairs and stopped to listen. Benson couldn't decide whether to follow or wait for his brother to clear the way.

"Mom, Dad, a bunch of kids are at Hamilton Memorial in the waiting room to find out about their friends, but also for Coach Rohart and Mrs. Matt. The guys really wanna be there. You know how Bennie feels about Mrs. Matt. I really think it'd help them to be part of it. There are several students in stable condition that can have visitors, too. And then there's the candlelight vigil after dark at Westwood. What do ya' think?"

Benson couldn't see his brother, but he could picture the innocent expression that concealed any of the reasons *Colin* wanted to go. *He's got more secrets than the CIA.*

"Oh, Colin, that's so sweet of you to help them. Tommy, what do you think? If they have friends at the hospital, I think they should be there, don't you?"

Benson peeked through the railing and saw his mom with papers spread all over the coffee table. His dad had converted the kitchen table into a temporary desk, pecking away on his laptop. He heard the clink of ice shifting in a glass as he pictured his dad sipping a scotch.

Can't do that at the office, I don't think.

"I think that's a great idea. Maybe we should join them, talk to the other parents. Keep your cell phone on vibrate, Colin, and we'll leave you a message when we plan to be there. I'd like us to have dinner together before the candlelight vigil. We'll get takeout or something, then we can go to the school. How's that sound?"

"Sure, Dad. You guys don't have to go, but I understand if you want to. Guys! C'mon!" Colin didn't bother coming back up. He had to know they were listening.

Benson grabbed Ryan's shirt sleeve, not wanting it to seem like they were right at the top of the stairs. After a few seconds, they plodded down them, Benson bracing for his mom's overcompensating hugs. He just wanted to get out of there. Not knowing about Mrs. Matt had him in knots.

"C'mere, honey." His mom saw the turmoil in his eyes and held him for several minutes. It embarrassed Benson for Ryan to see her doting over him, but her arms around him felt good.

"Thanks, Mom," he mumbled. She grabbed Ryan by the shoulder and hugged him with the other arm.

"You're welcome, honey. I love you." She let go of them both, but then held Benson at arm's length for a second. She brushed the bangs out of his eyes, then pressed her warm palm to his cheek for a second. Her eyes brimmed with tears.

"Love you, too." Benson's own eyes filled, but he made them stay. He was afraid if he started crying, he might not be able to stop.

"Don't be afraid to cry, Benson. There's nothing wrong with it, you hear me? Nothing at all. You boys have been through a terrible ordeal I can't even imagine. No kids should ever have to go through that." She patted both of them on the back, giving them the go-ahead to leave. Ryan half-waved and slipped out the front door. "We'll be there in just a bit."

"Bye, Mom. Bye, Dad." Benson paused for a second as both looked up at him. "And, uh, thanks for, you know, for everything."

"You're welcome, son." His dad looked touched, and the expression brought the lump back into Benson's throat.

"Oh, honey..." His mom came to the front door and gave him another hug. When she pulled away, tears slid down her cheeks. He gave as much of a smile as he could manage before he left.

"God, I thought she'd never let you go." Colin shuffled his keys and led the boys to the end of the driveway – the natural order of importance. Dad's SUV and Mom's Lexus side by side, then the banged-up '92 Mazda RX-7 that Colin treated like a Porsche Boxster. Ryan squeezed into the back so Benson could ride shotgun.

"Colin, you think maybe they should know about you and Megan? I mean, they're all worried about *me." And they should be worried about you,* Benson wanted to add, but he had made his point.

Colin revved his souped-up engine. "No time for that now, Bennie. There are more important things to take care of."

Benson fought the urge to glance back at Ryan as his

brother whipped out of the driveway. *Why is seeing Megan so important?* Benson was starting to get a better view of the big picture. And seeing a different side of his brother.

With Colin's wild driving, and flashbacks to the dream he *had* to share with Ryan, they arrived at the emergency room exit in less than ten minutes. Colin parked in the circle drive and put on his flashers. The sky blue Mazda didn't look as old it was, because Colin waxed it about as often as he brushed his teeth. So Colin leaving it like that surprised Benson.

On a day when he thought nothing could surprise him anymore.

Chapter 12

THE TWO YOUNGER boys had to practically jog down the hospital hallway to keep up with Colin. By the time they reached the elevator, he was holding the door for them.

"You two slow, or what?"

"Get a grip, Colin. Jesus," Benson muttered.

Colin scowled at him, a flash of the aggressive brother resurfacing. But Benson sensed those days had passed. Their fights seemed trivial now. Too much had happened to both of them, even though the weight of it couldn't be determined yet. Megan and Mrs. Matt might both make it and everything end up okay, guilt-free, even.

Please, Mrs. Matt...please. The idea that something awful could have happened to her sent his heart hammering.

As they headed toward the waiting room, Ryan whispered, "Did you see his hands, Ben. He's losing it, for real."

Ryan was right. Colin's hands had trembled noticeably when he hit the three button on the elevator. Then when he performed the age-old habit of scrubbing his hand through his hair, Benson saw the splotches of red on each cheek. He hadn't seen such a physical display of nervousness since Colin gave a speech for student council elections last school year.

What really happened between the two of you Saturday night, Colin? And which letter jacket story is true?

That debate was put on hold as they turned the corner into the waiting room. Benson and Ryan both balked at the sight of the Barbie Brigade. Nikki Harmon looked up and frowned at them. As one of their first interviewees, she might be making the connection. But then he might be giving her too much credit.

Would any of the others associate the rumors with their interviews? Releasing what Steve said to one person and then what that person said to yet someone else...it had been Benson's ploy to stir up the cappuccino. To show them there wasn't much distance from the bottom of the cup to the top.

It's not like I lied...

He shoved the possibilities aside, not wanting to acknowledge that, in some way, he might be an accessory to murder. Or at the very least the catalyst. He wondered for the millionth time if he could, or would, be charged with a crime.

Ryan snapped him out of his funk and pointed across the large waiting room at a TV hanging high in the far corner. It was muted, but an updated special bulletin about Westwood popped onto the screen, and no one had noticed. Benson marched across the room and turned up the volume. He joined Pam Utterbeck – who didn't have on nearly as much black make-up for some reason – and a few of their other friends. But the whole room was intermingled with various cliques. The only ones really separate were the Barbie Brigade, all holding each other and crying.

It was pretty much the same news report Benson and Ryan had seen earlier, but he didn't know if they'd heard it yet. When it finished, he muted it again. He felt an odd sense of power, not just because Colin had walked in with them. He couldn't put his finger on it, but everyone in the waiting room accepted his take-charge role of muting and unmuting the TV.

"I can't believe they would show the shell casings. Do you think that was blood in the hall?"

"I bet those were bullet holes in Principal Jacobsen's door," Ryan told Pam, who turned and told enough people that it circulated in minutes.

"That's where Steve took her," a familiar voice said. He saw everyone staring at someone over his shoulder. He turned to see Nikki Harmon with her arms crossed behind him.

She knows...she may be an airhead, but even pre-schoolers can connect the dots...

"Took who?" Pam asked.

"Megan. He took Megan into the office. *You* saw her, didn't you?" Nikki's red, puffy eyes glistened with fresh tears at Pam. "I heard you were in the office when it all happened."

"Yeah." Pam barely nodded. They all seemed to be joined by an invisible thread.

"That jerk pulled her in there like she was an animal." Nikki broke down and dropped into the seat by Benson. For a terrifying moment, he thought someone would expect him to put his hand on her shoulder or something. But the Barbie Brigade swooped in and whisked her back over to their corner. After a few minutes, they headed to the restroom just across the hall. Nikki's declaration made a few others cry, the mood in the room a hybrid of anger and sorrow.

"Mr. Barker!" Colin blurted, jumping to his feet. Benson's heart leapt into his throat as he watched his brother rush the man standing at the waiting room entrance. Mr. Barker had bags darker than Pam's mascara under his eyes.

"Colin," Mr. Barker said, shaking his brother's hand. "Thanks for coming."

"Sir, you think we could see her?" Colin looked too eager, almost fanatical. The hum in the room stopped.

"Our family is, um, well, just not now, okay?" The man sighed, a sound ragged with emotion. He had a deep crevice between his eyes. Was it deeper now than it was the day before?

Benson wondered.

"She would appreciate that all of you are here," Mr. Barker added, as tears filled his eyes. The whole room seemed to hold its breath waiting for him to either continue or break down. He couldn't know that many of them were there for other victims, especially the teachers. "Michael too." He let out a sob, wobbling before a doctor behind him offered an arm.

Oh, wow. Michael was one of them...

He turned to get Ryan's attention, but caught a glimpse of the redhead he'd seen on Friday instead – the cute cheer-leader. The sick feeling of getting busted for eavesdropping at the lockers surged through him again. But he couldn't stop staring.

I never looked her up in the yearbook...

"Will any of us get to see...her?" Nikki asked, her voice catching.

"Um, Megan, she...she can't have visitors," Mr. Barker muttered, and was gone before anyone else could speak. Not that they would've.

Mrs. Matt... Can she?

The doctor stepped into the room and held up a hand. "Sorry, Mr. Barker has had a rough day."

Before the doctor could leave, a small voice asked, "Can you tell us about the others?"

Everyone looked around the room to see who had spoken, and all eyes settled on Scooter, the seventh grader who liked to spew milk through his nose for a laugh.

The dark-headed physician, Alex Markum, Intern, his nametag read, draped a stethoscope around his neck, took a deep breath and said, "I can't tell you much yet. Ginny Rohart is down that hall with her husband, the coach." He pointed the opposite direction of Megan Barker's room. "And he's stable for now. Surgery went well. Mrs. Mattingly is in surgery now. Her husband and two kids are in a room just past Mr. Rohart's. We haven't been able to reach everyone's parents, but I can tell you what parents are here. It'll be up to them if they want visitors." The doctor shuffled papers on his clipboard.

All Benson could think about was Mrs. Matt. *Surgery... that's a good sign, right?* A wave of self-pity swept over him, so staggering he lost focus of the room. *God, if I caused you to get hurt, Mrs. Matt, I'm so sorry.* It was an irony Benson couldn't quite understand, but the vacuum sucking the air from his insides was enough.

The doctor rattled off names of families that meant nothing to him. But the cheerleaders broke into howling sobs, holding each other and blubbering names. A murmur ebbed through the room when the doctor finished the list with Thomas Silvey. Benson's stomach lurched.

"Is Tim okay?" Pam blurted.

"The Silveys are down in the other waiting room, and yes, it looks like Tim is going to be fine." The doctor looked behind him like he was measuring his escape route.

Other waiting room? Benson hadn't noticed one, but they had stopped at this one when they saw all their classmates.

"But you didn't say anything about Evan Anderson or Malakai Jeffries or Michael Barker." Nikki Harmon's voice was edged in panic. "Someone said they all got shot?"

It was a question, and from the look on the doctor's face, Benson knew she wasn't getting an answer.

"I can't tell you any more." The young physician shook his head.

He averted his gaze and started to add more when someone shouted, "Who died?"

"I'm sorry, that's a question for the police. I treat the living. Your principal and several others are in the other waiting room at the end of the hall. It will be up to them what else they want to share with you." The doctor started to back out of the room.

"Are the police here? So we can ask them?" Benson surprised himself by speaking. He felt Colin's stare, and he caught Mallorie looking at him. He didn't know why it made his ears turn red, but he made a point not to make eye contact with her.

"I would think so. Now if you'll excuse me... I'll notify your coach's wife and Mrs. Mattingly's husband. I will also tell the parents of the kids who can have visitors that you're all here." The doctor tapped his pen to a clipboard, then turned quickly and left.

No one said a word for several long moments, then the speculating started. Someone insisted Mrs. Matt and Coach Rohart had gotten shot right in front of the Media Center.

"And Mrs. Connors musta been the adult who died," Pam added.

Everyone nodded, comments coming from all around the room now.

"And I know for a fact that Malakai, Evan, and Michael got shot. It was like that's who Steve was looking for. So if they're not treating them, then they must be..." Randy raised his eyebrows, not willing to say it.

"Let's ask Dr. Jacobsen. He's cool. He'll tell us if he can," Pam suggested.

"Yeah, I'm in." Nikki and the rest of the Barbie Brigade stood, like they were ready to storm Ken's mansion.

Benson wanted to laugh, but a lump in his throat made him wonder if it would be tears that came instead. The Barbie Brigade had their back? *Or we have theirs...*

Without a word, the whole waiting room buzzed about what to do, to say. Benson started to say something to Ryan, but was floored to see Colin standing outside Megan's room with Mr. Barker. One moment they were gabbing, the next they both were disappearing into Room 317.

Holy crap.

"Yo, Bennie, what's got you by the shorthairs?" Ryan leaned forward to look Benson in the eye. But Benson couldn't tear his gaze from the door. While he stared at it, his brother came back out, followed by Mr. Barker.

What the hell are you doing, Colin?

He elbowed Ryan hard, who scanned the room for what had him so anxious. "No," Benson whispered. "*There.*"

Ryan followed his pointing finger.

"Oh, man," his best friend muttered.

"That's what I said. What should I do?" Benson whispered. Colin and Mr. Barker continued to talk. Both were crying. A doctor emerged from Megan's room and whispered something in Mr. Barker's ear, obviously too delicate to say in front of Colin. Benson stared at them, unable to take part in the conversations swirling around him.

Only about half of the students remained, most already on their way to the other waiting room.

"It was the steroids, man. That jerk was so juiced, it's a miracle he hadn't had an aneurysm. I hear they do that to you." A few others hanging around agreed.

Comments volleyed back and forth, debating that theory. But Benson continued to watch his brother right outside the waiting room, face to face with Mr. Barker like he had known the man all his life.

The doctor and Mr. Barker turned their backs on Colin to have a private word. Colin folded his arms across his chest, then dropped them, then stuffed his hands in his front jeans pockets. He gave a nervous glance over his shoulder at the students in the waiting room, but didn't lock eyes with anyone.

When the doctor left, Mr. Barker turned back to Colin, and the man's body language had shifted. His jaw was tight, his right hand clenching just before he started poking a finger in Colin's chest. His face had flushed crimson. His head bobbed angrily and spittle flew from his mouth. Colin's face turned equally red, and the vein on his forehead popped out like it did when he was totally ticked off and about to belt Benson over the head.

The conversation in the waiting room paused just as Colin shouted, "I'm not explaining jack *shit* to you! You wouldn't believe me if I told you. And that's between me and Megan anyway. It's nobody's damn business!"

The electricity in the waiting room pulsed, all eyes on Colin. Before Benson could get up, his brother threw a crumpled paper against Megan's door and bolted down the hallway toward the exit.

"THE POLICE ARE GONNA KNOW ABOUT THIS!" Mr. Barker boomed, looking around frantically before barging back into his daughter's room.

Chapter 13

"COLIN!" BENSON SHOUTED down the hospital stairwell, hearing the door to the floor below slam shut. *Where the hell are you going?*

He gripped the wadded note in his fist, not taking time to look at it, but he didn't dare leave it on the floor for the Barbie Brigade. *What could be in it that stoked Mr. Barker like that?*

Aching to know, he raced after his brother. Why had Colin gone soap opera all of a sudden? And what the heck had Mr. Barker meant about the police?

When he banged the door open on the second floor, he saw his brother slumped over in a hallway chair next to a tiny, wide-eyed boy clutching a *Get Well* balloon.

Colin glanced up as Benson neared him. "Leave me alone."

"No." Benson stood his ground. A new attitude had seized him since his near-death experience at Westwood less than eight hours earlier. And he and Colin were becoming the kind of brothers he'd always wanted. He wasn't backing down now.

The blunt answer made Colin look up again. "I'm not in the mood, Ben. Please."

"I know. I'm here to help, Colin. C'mon. You're acting so twisted, like you're...you're..." Benson froze. *No way.* "You're not doing drugs too, *are you?*"

"Ah, crap, Bennie. Hell, no. I'm not an idiot." Colin pressed his palms into his temples, gritted his teeth, and looked like he might scream. "This is just all so *bogus.*"

Benson didn't answer. He stuffed the note in his back pocket, then dropped into the empty seat between Colin and *Get Well* Boy. The pre-schooler scooted one seat away, wide-eyed like Benson might bite if provoked. He tried to smile at the shrimp, but he couldn't quite manage it. The kid slid off the chair and backed into the nearest room without ever turning his back on Benson.

Get a grip, kid. Just wait 'til you get to junior high.

"They're shutting off her life support. Can you believe that crap? One day – they won't even give her one lousy day." Emotion filled Colin's voice. "And...and that prick did this. I can't let him get away with it, Bennie. I can't."

"What're you gonna do? About the police and...and whatever else Mr. Barker's so fired up about." Benson was fishing for answers but didn't know how to come right out and ask.

"I...I don't know."

Benson couldn't see his brother's eyes, but as Colin bowed his head, tears dripped off the end of his nose onto the gray-flecked linoleum.

"Yes, I do." Colin jumped to his feet and wiped his face with the sleeve of his Henley shirt. "I'll be back, Ben. Go upstairs and keep me posted. Ah, crap, my cell's dead, I forgot. But...but I gotta run home for something. I'll be back for you and Ryan. Give me thirty minutes, okay?"

"Why can't I come with you?" Benson hated the desperate tone in his voice. "Never mind, it's all right. Ryan and I hafta finish some stuff anyway." *God, I sound so lame.*

He didn't want to turn into the kid brother who leeched after the god-like Colin Schmidt. It hadn't suited him for the past six years, so it wouldn't fit to start now. Though he liked what was happening between them.

"Thanks. And, if anyone asks, tell 'em...tell 'em... Oh, hell, I don't care what you tell them. After seeing Megan, nothing matters. Not anymore." Colin shoved his hands in his front jeans pocket and headed down the hall, more determined than earlier but with none of his usual *I'm Colin Schmidt, by God* swagger.

Benson watched him go, feeling even more like he was in the middle of a made-for-TV movie. Cryptic answers to vague questions and too many plot twists to keep up. M. Night Shyamalan couldn't direct anything crazier. He and Colin loved his movies even more than Spielberg's.

Christ, this is out of control.

After a few minutes, he made his way back toward the

waiting room, wondering what he would say to the information-hungry masses. He could make up stories with the best of them, but he didn't have to bother. As soon as he turned the corner out of the stairwell and walked past the nurse's station, he heard the TV blaring. The waiting room was full again. The Barbie Brigade and all their followers had returned while he was gone.

"...and will be held until further notice. Jamestown has joined the infamous ranks among the worst of the school shootings with Columbine, Santana, and Red Lake. The death toll at this hour is fourteen, and this tragic day is not over for the small city. We've just received word that a teacher and another student have died..."

Benson froze just inside the waiting room and stared at the TV in the far corner. The scene went to a reporter standing at the circle drive of the hospital. If Benson had gone to the window, he would be able to look down and see her in the flesh.

"I'm here at Hamilton Memorial Hospital with Dr. Jim Jacobsen, Westwood Junior High's principal. Dr. Jacobsen, I know this has been a very painful day..."

Painful? Tears jammed around the angry wedge in his throat.

His principal responded to the lame comment, then answered the first questions without emotion. He emphasized the heroic efforts of teachers and students in saving lives, and thanked law enforcement for being quick and instrumental in bringing the whole tragedy to a close.

"We understand that your school has lost twelve students, a secretary, and one teacher. With that number, Westwood has surpassed Columbine in fatalities. And much like the Colorado high school, you lost a beloved teacher today." The reporter shoved the microphone into Dr. Jacobsen's face, and the whole room held its breath.

No...

Benson wanted to run, anything but listening to this.

"Yes, Mia, I..." The principal had to clear his throat, his eyes suddenly full of tears. "A veteran teacher, Elaine

Mattingly, just passed away, and she is single-handedly responsible for saving a young girl's life this morning." Dr. Jacobsen's voice trembled, and though it looked like he wanted to say more, he shook his head. He couldn't.

Benson reached blindly behind him for a seat and made his way into it. A clog filled his throat. Kids in the waiting room burst into tears, some sobbing and others babbling about how much they loved Mrs. Matt.

Benson buried his face in his hands and bawled.

He cried so hard, his head throbbed. But he couldn't stop. He'd never known anyone who had died before. His grandmother passed away when he was two, but he didn't remember her or her funeral.

Oh, God, funerals...

That brought on fresh tears, the idea of mourning Mrs. Matt, of seeing her in a casket. Sobs made his head and stomach hurt, snot streaming across his upper lip. He fumbled out the door to the men's room, blindly grabbing paper towels to blow his nose. When he could see, he slipped into a stall, unrolled toilet paper, and blew it again.

He stayed in the bathroom for several minutes, not wanting to go back, not wanting to feel the sorrow that cloaked the waiting room, and not wanting to explain to anybody why there was a massive void inside him. He didn't just miss Mrs. Matt, though he had adored her.

He felt responsible.

If it hadn't been for Operation Cappuccino, none of this would've happened. As much as he didn't want to believe that, he couldn't help it. Self-pity swallowed him, and he had no reason to deny it.

The door opened, and he jumped, grabbing more toilet paper to wipe his face.

"Hey, Ben. You okay?"

His mouth nearly fell open. Mallorie had entered no-woman's land to see where he had gone.

To check on me...

"I...uh...yeah. I mean, no. I..." But the tears threatened to break the dam again. *Don't embarrass yourself...*

She inched inside, letting the door close but looking around nervously. "I know. I really liked Mrs. Matt, too. They said she saved a student's life today. We should be proud..." Mallorie lowered her head.

"Proud?" Benson's chest filled with rage. He didn't like the way it made him feel, but it engulfed him like a fueled fire. "That my favorite teacher died? That some idiot brought a gun to school because he...he figured out that he wasn't God's gift? That I..." Benson stopped, the tirade withering as fast as it had surged. *I what?* He didn't put that gun in Steve's hand, didn't drive him to hate, and didn't pull the trigger.

So why do I feel like crap?

He looked up and saw the shock on Mallorie's face. She mumbled something too low to understand and backed out, letting the door close between them. Benson lunged for it and caught her just outside the door.

"Oh, hey, Mallorie. I...I, uh, I'm really sorry. You just kinda hit a nerve, I guess."

She turned to face him. "I have a knack for that. And I do understand how you feel – most of it anyway. I didn't know Mrs. Matt too well, but Megan was one of my closest friends." Her face pinched like she might cry.

Benson took another step toward her. Before he knew what he was doing, he held her while she cried. He was only an inch or two taller, and her wavy golden hair smelled like flowers. Her hands rested on the small of his back and her body trembled as she cried.

In another world, Benson Schmidt would be on cloud nine, but not today.

When she finally let go, she brushed tears away, apologized, but grinned sheepishly at him. Benson stuffed his hands in his pockets.

"It's been a horrible day." He glanced up and saw Ryan and Pam staring at him from the waiting room.

"I...I gotta get back," Mallorie mumbled, her voice thick from crying.

"Me, too." *I think I just started the Cappuccino machine... or blew it up.*

Benson walked with her to the waiting room, and she headed to her pack of friends. Ryan and Pam gawked at him as he plopped into the seat between them.

"What was *that* all about?" Ryan asked, and Pam added, "Barbie break a nail?"

"No... She...she just wanted to vent, I guess," Benson mumbled. *Have I crossed to the dark side? This was what we wanted, right? Then why do I feel like a traitor?*

Ryan sighed, hopefully letting it go for now. "Where's Colin?"

"Ran home for something. He said he'd be back in about thirty minutes. Acted really strange, too. I can't even imagine what Mom and Dad are going to say when he shows up without us. He's gone mental, Ryan. They're going to send him to Havenwood Mental Health, for real."

"What'd he say about Mr. Barker? And that note?" Ryan fidgeted, and Benson knew what his best friend wanted.

"They're considering turning off her life support, and he's totally pissed about it. I gave him the note back, but I don't think he really wanted it," Benson lied, not sure why he was doing it.

"Man, I wanted to read it," Ryan said, his eyes narrowing as he stared at Benson.

He doesn't believe me. Have I ever lied to Ryan? If he had, he couldn't remember it, except the time he denied eating boogers in first grade.

"You wanna go to the other waiting room? See what they know?" Ryan sat up and leaned forward, looking from Benson to Pam.

"Nah, I think I'll just stay here. I...I just can't believe about Mrs. Matt." Benson buried his face in his hands.

"Want me to stay?" Ryan whispered, his voice husky with emotion.

"No, go ahead. I'll be okay." Benson glanced up, his eyes blurry. But he couldn't mistake the uncertainty in his best friend's expression. *I'm not trying to get rid of you. I just want to be alone.*

Ryan and Pam left, both glancing back several times before

turning the corner. He considered going to sit by Mallorie, but for now, he just needed to think. He gave a half wave as he exited the waiting room, and she smiled and waved back. Slipping into the stairwell, Benson let the tears come. Hating the lump of emotion that wouldn't let go of him, he scrambled down the stairs. Tears blurred his vision as he took them two at a time, frantic for air and no walls. One slip and he would splat to the bottom, but he didn't care. He hadn't bargained for any of this – the shooting, Mallorie, lying to his best friend...or Mrs. Matt.

What the hell have I done? Benson finally made it to the emergency room exit and gulped fresh air seconds before he vomited in the bushes. When the heaves passed, he dropped onto the plush grass away from the entrance, plucking one blade at a time and trying to process what the past eight hours had done to his world.

Twenty minutes later when Colin got back, Benson had a grass igloo, but no answers.

"The Diva Diary"

Some of these people being here make me sick. They're like vultures, aren't they? ~ Lady Di

Yeah, but maybe they're here for people we don't know. We're still not sure who all got shot. It sucks being here like this anyway. I just want to go home. ~ Em

I want to see Megan. I just know that asshole shot her. I know it. Why else were so many of US hurt? ~ Opal

Yeah, why couldn't he have gone postal on the Nerd Herd? Who would've cared? I mean, really? ~ Lady Di

I can't believe you said that... ~ Jade

That is truly awful, Nikki. You don't really believe that, do you??? I mean, come on! ~ Skye

NO NAMES, Skye, God, are you trying to reserve a room in ISD for the rest of the year? ~ Lady Di

Sorry... But that's scary to hear you say that. Some of our classmates are dead and many are in intensive care. And look around you...a bunch are like, borderline Havenwood, you know? Now's not the time to put people down. It's not right. ~ Skye

Okay, girls, enough bickering. Sitting in a waiting room is driving us all crazy, but we have to stick together now more than ever. Megan, sorry, Amey needs us. And if Steroid Boy is responsible, then we must tell what we know. Right? ~ Em

I'm not telling anybody about that. Not now, not ever. If you want to, go right ahead. But I promised. And how horrible would it be to tell now? ~ Skye

I agree. If it becomes an issue, we'll write an anonymous letter or something. But she's going to be fine. She HAS to be fine. ~ Opal

We need to do something... Don't we? ~ Jade

Let's stay strong for Amethyst. It's our oath, remember? The gems have to stick together, so we all agree. Our lips are sealed? ~ Lady Di

Yes. ~ Opal

Yes. ~ Em

I guess so. ~ Jade

I'm in, too. ~ Skye

Well the decision is final, and we know he'll get his. His kind always does. ~ Lady Di

Chapter 14

"I'VE GOTTA SEE Mr. Barker, but I'll be back." Colin never slowed, dashing by Benson without asking what he was doing outside.

Benson jumped up to follow, then stopped. He didn't want to go back in there. The place overwhelmed him with death and all the crap that went with it.

The note!

He plucked the paper from his back pocket and dropped next to his pile of plucked grass. He unfolded it carefully, as the thrill of *knowing* sliced through.

Colin,

I'm sooooooo stressed. Steve just went tearing out of school, and I think he knows what happened between us. I would've NEVER told him, but u know there were things I would never do with him. Well, u know, I told u about those times.

Benson blinked, horrified by the idea that Megan had written this the day of the shooting.

I admit I worry about things like STDs, but you know my biggest fear. My God, my parents would go like totally postal.

I tried to call your cell, but u must've it turned off. When Steve stormed out of the office, he yelled, right in front of the Dr. Jacobsen, "You'll pay for this, bitch! Nobody touches my girl...nobody." He thinks he owns me, like I'm just property or something. What r we gonna do? He's been suspended for 10 days and I think Coach kicked him off the team. Maybe they finally know about some of the stuff he's been doing. I can't imagine what he'll be like if he can't play football. It's his life.

I really need to talk to u. I hate it when u turn off your phone. I'll try again in a few minutes. Love you... Megan

"Dang." Benson reread the note three times, refolded it neatly, then flipped open his cell phone. He didn't have to go upstairs to get Ryan's input. He hit speed dial number one and cringed when it went to voice mail. *C'mon, Ryan, pick up.* He tried again, but each time, the call went straight to voice mail. *Either he's got it turned off, or he's trying to figure out why I'm sleazing with the enemy.*

Benson didn't know what to do. For ten solid minutes, he stared at cars passing by, wondering how many of them had the same gagging blob in their throats.

Could someone live in our town and not know about the shooting? Is that possible? He decided only if they didn't listen to the radio, watch TV, talk to their friends and neighbors, and boycotted newspapers.

Squinting at a Hummer coasting by, imagining himself behind the wheel and barreling down Westwood's halls in it, Benson jumped when Colin stormed out the emergency room exit.

"Let's go," his brother snapped, Ryan jogging to keep up.

The three boys piled into the RX-7 without saying anything else. Benson ached to find out what Ryan had learned in the other waiting room and wanted to share the note with his best friend. But Colin's heavy foot and the dark cloud surrounding him silenced both younger boys.

Benson even forgot to worry about Ryan's response to the Mallorie factor. To ease the anxiety plaguing him, he asked, "Where are we going?"

"We've got some loose ends to tie up." Colin barely slowed

for a stop sign at the end of Hospital Drive. "Been a weird day, huh?"

Ryan grunted. "Way. When I left Pam Utterbeck in the waiting room, she was actually talking to Mallorie Taylor about abortion – and they were *agreeing.*"

Benson's face flushed, imagining Mallorie's bright eyes, her smile, her dimples. *If Pam and Mallorie became friends, that would be the point, wouldn't it?.*

Colin skidded to a stop for a red light, then lurched forward inches at a time until the light changed. Obviously testing the car's ability to go from zero to sixty in mere seconds, he burned rubber and sent Benson's heart hammering.

Oh, man... Déjà vu pulsed through him as they headed downtown – toward Broadway and 47th.

He gripped the handle on the door so tight his knuckles ached.

As if he knew, Colin nearly doubled the speed limit as they wheeled onto Broadway. His heavy foot sent them racing toward the dreaded intersection.

Images of the dream overlapped with his current reality, overloading Benson's already tired brain.

"What's the matter with you?" Colin asked. "You look like you did that time you ate lima beans."

"I'm fine." Benson squirmed. Seeing the intersection race toward him like a swirling tornado forced enough bile into his throat to choke him. He swallowed hard as Colin sped up. *I wish I'd told Ryan...he'll never believe me now.*

"Slow down," he muttered.

"Ah, relax, little bro, I'm NASCAR's wet dream." Colin's wild-eyed expression had Benson near panic. He couldn't stand it anymore and finally glanced back at Ryan, who looked terrified and confused. Their eyes met, and Benson cast a glance at the road, then at Colin, telepathy for *He's gonna kill us.*

Ryan nodded but couldn't seem to manage anything more. Benson closed his eyes as they barreled through the intersection. When he could tell they were through it, he let out the breath he hadn't realized he was holding – no crash, no chair splintered into a million bits, no decapitated Colin.

"Why won't you tell us where we're going?" Benson finally asked, when he had calmed down enough. He watched the road, too afraid not to. But with the deadly intersection behind him, at least he could concentrate now.

"You'll see, Bennie, you'll see." Colin darted into the light traffic. He squealed his tires turning onto Wehmeyer, barely stopping in time for a red light, then peeled out again.

Oh my God...you're gonna kill us.

Then it hit him. He didn't know exactly where the Barkers lived, but he knew it was around the Country Club and that was exactly where they were headed. Benson turned to Ryan and gave an open-mouthed *I get it* expression. From Ryan's knitted brow, it was obvious he hadn't had the revelation yet.

"You can't go there, Colin. I don't know why you would want to. Think hard before you do anything stupid." Benson stared at his brother. What had Mr. Barker meant in the hospital? Why *was* Colin being so mysterious?

Colin turned and took a long hard gaze at the younger Schmidt, so long that Benson watched the road in frantic anticipation. His nerves jangled.

Look where you're going!

Finally, Colin did. But Benson got the bigger picture.

He doesn't care if he dies... Maybe my dream was a crazy premonition.

When the Mazda pulled between massive iron gates with an ornate B embossed in the middle, Ryan grabbed Benson's sleeve from the back seat.

Now he gets it. Benson suppressed a laugh.

"I want my jacket," Colin stated matter-of-factly. He parked in front of the biggest house Benson had ever seen.

"Wouldn't your jacket be at school? Or at the hospital? Or the police may even have it. Besides, Colin, there's probably nobody here."

"Ramona dropped off Megan's stuff, remember? My jacket better be here. If not, we're going to the hospital next. Wait here."

Ryan and Benson sat stunned for the first full minute after

Colin exited the car. They watched him approach the front door, speak to someone who answered, and then slip nonchalantly inside.

"Jesus, what the hell is he doing?" Ryan finally asked. Benson fought the urge to divulge his lie, to pull the note from his back pocket, but things were too weird to add to the drama.

"I don't know, but there's more to this. He's really goin' off the deep end."

"I can never figure your brother out. I think he gets a kick out of making people wonder what the heck he's up to."

"Something's not right." Benson stared at the front door, wishing it would open and they could get out of there.

"Being here feels wrong. What if Mr. Barker drove up right now?" Ryan asked.

Benson turned just as Ryan did, making sure the driveway was still empty. "He knows better. They won't leave Megan's side."

They chatted, trying to take it all in. They even replayed the day, what each had been thinking during the shooting. Nearly thirty minutes passed before Colin finally emerged with his letter jacket draped over his left arm.

"Looky there. It's like destroying evidence, isn't it?" Benson watched Colin strut to the car with a gleam in his eye.

"Hey, guys. Sorry it took so long. I've been gabbin' with Ramona. She bakes a mean brownie. Says she cooks when she's stressed. Here, try one." Colin tossed the jacket into the backseat next to Ryan and handed Benson a napkin with four enormous, gooey brownies on it. The smell of chocolate filled the small sports car.

The younger boys didn't move at first. Colin's glib indifference gave Benson chills.

"Go on, take 'em. They're great. Sorry I didn't getcha any milk. We can stop if you got any green."

Benson shook his head, knowing that despite healthy allowances, neither he nor Ryan ever had money on them. He had over three hundred dollars in the bank but not a dime in his pocket.

Colin took one of the brownies and passed it back to Ryan,

who oohed and ahhed. The smell of chocolate stirred Benson's uncertain stomach, but just staring at the brownie made his mouth sticky with the desire for milk.

"If we're going to eat these, you've gotta drive normal or I'm gonna puke in your precious car." Benson took a small bite of one of the brownies, balancing the remaining one on his lap.

He goes into his comatose girlfriend's house to take back his letter jacket and returns with brownies. Damn.

Benson savored another bite, rolling the chocolate on his tongue. He was trying to think how to ask Colin why getting the jacket had been so pressing.

Remarkably, Colin pulled out of the driveway and eased onto Broadway this time without squealing tires, the relief evident not only in his driving but on his face.

That jacket meant that much to him? Why?

They pulled into a Git 'n Go and, before Ryan or Benson could say a word, Colin was out of the car and standing at the counter with a quart of milk in his hand.

"Why's he being so nice to us?" Benson watched his alien brother pay.

"I don't know, but him goin' after that jacket is just weird."

"Yeah." Benson glanced back at the treasured Jamestown High black jacket with gold leather sleeves. The giant J was already decorated with gold bars from Colin's freshman year playing varsity. "Anything in the pockets?"

Benson watched Colin, shielding his eyes from the late afternoon sun, then looked back at Ryan as his best friend carefully reached into the first pocket. Just as he pulled his hand out and started to feel inside the other one, Colin emerged from the store.

"*Stop!*" Benson hissed, not daring to say it louder with the windows down. He couldn't see Ryan, but he could picture his best friend's panicked expression. There would be two bright red spots on each cheek. It was a reaction Ryan could never prevent.

For the next forty-five minutes, the three boys drove the cruise route, finishing the brownies and drinking milk out of the carton.

Horns honked, hands waved, and Colin's name was shouted from many of the passing cars. Drivers were probably a little more subdued than normal, but teenagers still had the need for normalcy, Benson supposed. For a few fleeting moments, he understood what it felt like to be carefree and popular. And much to his surprise, he liked it. The revelation filled him with guilt.

How can these people cruise after what happened today?

"Are we going to the vigil?" Benson checked his watch. "We're supposed to go home for dinner, don't forget. It's almost six."

"Hey, call Mom and Dad and tell 'em we're gonna grab a burger with friends then go on to the school. I don't feel like playing the parent game right now. After those brownies, I'm not hungry anyway. Are you guys?"

Benson's mouth fell open before muttering no. Colin never shared what he felt about anything, especially their parents. *Is he using us?*

"Think they'll mind?" Benson never lied to his parents about anything. He conveniently omitted things, but that felt different. His heart raced.

"I'll call mine and tell them where I am. I said I'd be home by dinner, so they may say no." Ryan pulled his cell from his pocket and dialed.

Benson waited for advice from Colin, who was obviously more practiced at deceiving. "Are you going to ditch us somewhere?"

"Nah. Why would I? Just showin' you the ropes, you know, to see what's in your future – cruising and being seen by everybody you want to be seen by."

"Oh, I get it. I'm a loser, so you're going to show me what it would feel like to be you?" The ugly monster awakened inside him, the one that swallowed him during many after-school fights.

"Jesus, Bennie, that's not what I meant. And you're not a loser. You've just chosen to be a dork. I mean, is that for real? Do you really like sitting in the back of the lunchroom? I don't get that. How can a little brother of mine be so freakin' smart, but so dumb all at the same time? It's about *sway.*"

Benson stared long and hard at his brother. How many times had he idolized that face, that profile? When had it changed into jealousy and resentment? And what was happening now? Were he and Colin meeting somewhere in the middle? He didn't dare believe that, not in one day. Colin was apt to transform into Darth Vader in the next minute and a half.

"Sway?" he finally asked.

"You know, that 'it' factor. When you got it, you don't wait in line, you don't hafta ask for stuff...people just give it to you. It's just a belief in yourself."

Ryan muttered, "Yeah, if you're six foot and got game."

Could I have it if I wanted it? He hated that he wondered about it now. What the heck did that mean? Instead of mentally venturing into that taboo world of *wanting,* he changed the subject. "How long do you think we'll be outta school?"

Ryan flipped his phone shut. "Mom wants me home. Sorry, guys."

"Well, let's just eat with the parents then." Colin zipped into a parking lot to turn around. "And I think you'll be outta school at least until next week. That's my guess, anyway. At Columbine, they didn't go back the rest of the year, I don't think. I bet you don't go to Westwood when you go back anyway. They have to repaint and everything. You might go to Parkway or something."

"You're kidding." Benson tried to imagine what it would be like to go to a different school, to walk different halls and stare at different faces. *It would be better than walking into our Media Center.*

"Wow, I never dreamed we'd be out more than a few days." Ryan handed the milk to Benson and let out a window-rattling burp.

"Dang, Ryan, that's a good one." Colin honked and waved at someone, but Benson noticed he did it all without smiling.

He's puttin' on a show, trying to get back to normal.

A few minutes later, they pulled into Ryan's driveway.

"Hey, call me in the morning, okay?" Benson had stepped out so Ryan could weasel out of Colin's tiny backseat.

"Sure." Ryan half-waved as he headed up the driveway. "If they say I can go to the vigil, I'll call you guys. If you want me to," he added as he walked toward his two-story colonial house.

"Definitely," Benson said, hoping the lie hadn't caused a rift, either through his own guilt or Ryan's reaction when he confessed about the note.

As they headed home, he thought about telling Colin what happened with Mallorie. He could even admit to having the note. But then Colin might be pissed he'd read it in the first place.

After only two or three minutes, Colin blurted, "Megan and Steve were already on the outs, you know." He didn't look over at Benson, but continued, talking more to himself. Benson held his breath, caught off guard by his brother's sudden trust. "Before the fights, I mean. Ryan said you two were inter-viewing the jocks and repeated some comments Steve had made about cheerleaders. He thought you two had stoked the fire. But there's *way* more to it than that."

"Really?" Benson's stomach lurched. Operation Cappuccino might not be to blame for the shooting? Barbells lifted from his shoulders.

"Yeah. I guess you figured out about me and Megan." Colin paused, but Benson didn't utter the *duh* he was thinking. "We started going out about seven weeks ago. Hit it off big time, and we've been keeping it secret. She told Steve two weeks ago she was seeing someone else and that it was over. He knew it was true, but hearing it sent him over the edge. I guess that's an understatement. And the funniest thing is, he said no. Just like that, he said no. Like he owned her or something."

"That's how his kind think, Colin. You should know that." He stared at his brother's perfect profile. Benson had the same good looks. He knew girls looked at him, had even heard a few say *what a waste*. But Mallorie had noticed him, hadn't she? It made his stomach flip again just thinking about it.

They were nearly home when Colin's jaw stiffened. "I'm not

like Steve. *You* should know *that*, Benson. Being popular doesn't make us all stuck-up. Devin is my best friend, and even though he's a decent tailback, most people don't even know him. He doesn't talk with much of anybody but me or Jase. So he's not exactly Mr. Popularity."

Benson didn't know who was hip in Colin's class. He always assumed Devin was popular by association. It struck him odd that classmates wouldn't like Devin because of Colin. But he'd never heard the Barbie Brigade make google eyes over Devin like they did when they hero-worshipped other upper classmen, like Colin. "So you're tellin' me you hang out with dregs?"

"With what?" Colin half-chuckled.

"Dregs. You know, bottom feeders, outcasts. People who don't really mix with the other cliques." Benson felt a weird shame fill him. So many were forced to be dregs. *I don't mix because I don't want to...*

"I've never heard it called that before, but yeah... I don't hang out with people based on reputation. I hang out with my friends. Some since first grade, like Jase. One guy, Petey Tanner, just moved here this summer. He's pretty fun to be with, and he's kind of a skater, or – or maybe a metal head. But we like him. He's a riot."

"But don't you think they're popular just because you hang out with 'em, Colin?"

"Obviously not. If so, Devin would have a girlfriend. So you're wrong about some of us."

"Well, you and I don't exactly get along most of the time. This is the most we've talked since I was two." Benson tried to laugh to ease the comment. But they both knew it was true.

"I just like razzin' you. You get so fired up about it. I don't mean it half the time, but it's fun to pick on you." Colin glanced at Benson. "Why're you grinning?"

"I'm not sure why you're being so nice." Benson watched his brother's expression change as Colin pulled into their neighborhood.

"I'm sorry if I haven't been nice to you. It'd be a crummy time not to be, don'tcha think?"

"Yeah," Benson murmured.

Does that mean things will be back to normal by next week? He didn't ask, because he didn't want to know the answer.

* * *

The Mazda cruised smoothly down Valsuvia Boulevard. The late summer heat still soaked the air with humidity. Benson let his arm dangle out the car window, thinking how incredibly hot it was, but the chill he felt deep inside wouldn't go away. He was relieved when Colin pulled into their driveway.

When they walked in, the maddening smell of the grill made Benson's stomach growl.

His mom and dad swept them into the dining room where they hadn't eaten since Easter. Sit-down dinners at the table – sometimes from take-out containers – were a once-a-week affair, but never on a weekday. And never in the formal dining room.

Benson sat back and let himself enjoy the attention. His apprehension at going to the vigil in a few hours kept him from completely relaxing, but dinner was nice.

Their dad had grilled a sirloin, their mom had steamed fresh green beans, made baked potatoes piled with everything the way he liked them, and she had even made brownies. Both boys stifled a grin but didn't say a word. When they sat down to eat, Benson was caught off guard by his dad saying grace. That was once a year, if ever.

There are a lot of people who need praying for...one might be at the table with us now.

Benson stared at his brother directly across from him and wondered if things would ever be the same. He knew going back to school would be hard, but could he imagine how Colin felt?

Yes, I can... Mrs. Matt's face sucker-punched him.

"You make good grades, most of the kids like you, and you're handsome. Quite frankly, you're a walking contradiction..."

He swallowed hard. Had Mrs. Matt been right? What had she thought – really thought – about him, especially when he and Ryan proposed *Operation Cappuccino?* It swelled the gorge in his throat that he'd never know.

He stared at his plate as his dad mumbled, "Amen."

"So," his dad started, as if they could talk about the weather or the Colts' chances of getting Peyton another Super Bowl ring.

Benson looked up and saw that his parents were staring at him.

It's him you should be worried about. He took a quick look at Colin, whose face had whitened to a shade barely darker than the tablecloth. Megan hadn't died yet, but the clock was ticking.

Benson fought the urge to tell them, to break the barrier between teenager and adult, but realized with sick horror that it didn't matter anymore. They couldn't flip on the light and make the sniveling green monster under his bed go away.

The world had turned inside out and upside down, to the point that teenagers were committing adult crimes, and parents couldn't shelter their kids from the crappy reality of it.

More than anything, Benson wanted to crawl under the bed with the monster. At least then he could see it coming.

Chapter 15

BENSON SAT ON the lawn in front of their school, squinting at Ryan in the darkening dusk. Pinpoints of light from the few twinkling candles confused his eyes, adjusting to the twilight. Crickets chattered, too stupid to know it wasn't okay to be chirpy. Cars lined the streets or pulled into the teacher parking lot, and too many idiots crept by, rubbernecking.

All of it made his skin crawl. That eerie surge of anger burned from his groin to his ears. *Who the hell did Steve Ralston think he was?* The heat deepened. He gritted his teeth, felt a rage he'd never known before pulse through him.

"Benson?"

The emotion snapped, caved in on him with suffocating pressure.

"You okay?" Ryan waved a hand in front of his face, blurry around the edges but it was Ryan. He'd know those freckles anywhere.

As the moment evaporated, Benson wondered what was happening to him. But deep down, he knew...if Mrs. Matt died, he was responsible, wasn't he? The idea of it terrified him.

He could hate Ralston, but he'd have to hate himself, too.

"Dude, you're like bright red. What's up?" Ryan laughed, but it didn't sound too heartfelt.

"I...I..." *I what?* He continued plucking grass, his new favorite hobby, as they sat near the Westwood Junior High sign. *One of the nation's leading schools, my ass.*

Instead of trying to explain his mood, he gave Ryan an abridged version of the dream.

"So what do you think it means?" he asked when he finished.

He was glad Ryan had called – he couldn't imagine coming to the vigil alone, no matter how nice Colin was being or that his parents had insisted on chauffeuring them. He still felt alone around them. Ryan was the only one who knew how he felt.

"I don't know. It's weird. All of this is weird." Ryan waved his hand at the fifty or sixty students gathered between the circle drive and the street, none of their friends in the mix yet. His mom and dad had migrated to a gathering of adults. "Why does it take crap like this to bring people together?"

Benson shrugged. He stared at the adults. They could never understand what it had been like.

...to almost die...to feel the crushing guilt...

Darkness was blanketing the area, and candles began casting flickering glows on faces, making everyone's tears glisten. He refused to cry any more, to give into the suffocating pressure in his chest.

People knelt in front of the memorial surrounding the lying sign. How could they even stand to look at it?

Nation's Leading Schools...what a load of crap.

He felt the surge again. He wanted to kick it as hard as he could, take a hammer to it. But that didn't stop mourners from leaving flowers, stuffed animals, and cards around it. Many adults and teenagers wept openly, and every sniffle tugged at his heart.

He tried not to look at the pictures of Ralston's victims... some taped to the stupid sign, others propped against it. A large poster of Mrs. Connors had piles of flowers and cards around it. Another one just at the far edge had twice as many bouquets, teddy bears, and sympathy notes. But Benson wouldn't look. They couldn't make him, and the fist squeezing his heart wouldn't change his mind.

"Colin..." he murmured, not sure why he cared.

"Over there." Ryan head-pointed toward some athletes in various letter jackets – several Jamestown Yellow Jackets, even some Parkway South Panthers. Colin was one of the few not in a jacket.

I don't blame him for not wearing it...

"Not sure being a jock is top of the food chain today. I guess that's why they're way over there," Ryan added.

"I wouldn't be caught dead in one of those..." Benson sucked in his breath, realizing what he'd said. His hand hovered over his grass pile that now looked strangely like another green igloo. *Was that symbolic for something?*

"How do they wear 'em when it's so freakin' hot anyway?" Ryan flicked a ladybug from the front door of his igloo. "Think your mom's right, that he'll get a change of venue?"

"I don't know." Benson didn't want to talk about Ralston, didn't like the idea of adding fuel to the frenzy. His mom thought she would be asked to sit second chair. Would this be the case that got her the promotion she wanted?

He shivered. It made him sick that his pain, his guilt could help his mother achieve everything she'd worked for.

Colin wandered over to them and dropped in front of their grass piles. The dark circles under his eyes made him look haunted, like a ghost. He leaned toward Benson, his breath pungent. Alcohol?

God, I don't even know you.

"I know why he did it." Colin gave a weak grin, then stood and sauntered back toward the other letter jackets.

"Whoa..." Shivers rippled down Benson's back.

"Do you think he really knows?" Ryan sounded almost envious.

"Why can't Mom and Dad see it?" Benson watched his parents wander closer to the memorial, along with everyone else. It was almost completely dark.

Pam Utterbeck cackled as she approached them, making some sarcastic comment that Benson couldn't quite understand. He scowled. *Not here, Pam...* She had foregone her black eyeliner, though every stitch of clothing blended into the darkening night, as well as the netting on her hands.

They hopped up and followed her and the other students who had begun to gather closer to the memorialized sign. Benson still wanted to bash in the *leading* and paint *crappy* or *bloody* or something more fitting.

Parents layered behind them as a reverend asked them to bow their heads and led them in prayer. Everyone held hands as the last hint of sunset disappeared behind the trees. A school counselor handed out more candles. Dr. Jacobsen lit his and started the circle of neighbors passing the flame along to the next person.

He found Colin in the crowd, but his brother made eye contact with no one. *What're you thinking about, Colin?* How could his parents not see it? His mom was a freakin' lawyer!

Mom and Dad have gotta see how bad he's...

A knife lasered through his insides to see Ms. Waters step forward with a crumpled sheet of paper in her hands. Colin wasn't the only one hurting.

She cleared her throat and wiped tears from her cheeks. She scanned the crowd, her puffy, red-rimmed eyes sending an empathetic twinge through Benson.

"This has been a tragic day for Westwood and Jamestown," she said, her voice thick with emotion. "We're here to honor those we lost today..." Her bottom lip trembled.

Benson twitched. He wanted to race to Ms. Waters and hug her, tell her it was all his fault. He took one step, then another. He felt everyone's eyes on him, a few whispers, but he had to make things right.

Ryan yanked him backward as Dr. Jacobson stepped forward and began reading names.

"Are you nuts?" Ryan whispered.

Dr. Jacobson paused between names. Benson cringed every time someone sobbed or groaned.

"Malakai Jeffries, Evan Anderson. Michael Barker. Tyler Leslie." His principal's voice droned on, but the instant Benson heard the secretary's name, he knew what was next. "...and Mrs. Elaine Mattingly." Dr. Jacobson stopped, wiped tears streaming down his face.

Benson's stomach clamped. For a moment, blinded by tears, he wanted to throw himself on the ground and scream for everyone to *go AWAY*. How could they miss her more than he did?

I'm so sorry, Mrs. Matt...

He fisted away the tears and tried to swallow the sobs that made each breath hitch. The fist clenched tighter inside his chest. He couldn't breathe...didn't want to, really. His mom rubbed his back, like that would make anything better. *DON'T TOUCH ME!* he wanted to scream. But the principal continued speaking, like words could make any damn difference.

Mr. Baillargeon, Ms. Waters, and several other teachers joined the principal in the center. "And these people are in need of our prayers." Dr. Jacobson started reciting names. When he announced Megan Barker's, a girl broke down, and Benson searched for Colin. "And... I'm pleased to tell you Coach Rohart will make a full recovery."

The crowd broke into spontaneous applause that startled Benson. *They're clapping?* He understood the need for good news, but that didn't stop it from pissing him off.

The vigil continued for almost an hour before Benson told his parents he was ready to go. He and Ryan followed them to the teacher lot where they'd parked.

"Hey! Son, can I ask you a few questions?" A reporter for Channel 7 came running at them.

Benson looked around to see who the guy meant. "Me?" he asked.

"Yeah. Were you there today? Did you see anything?" The reporter shoved a microphone in his face.

"Hey, mister, get back." His dad stepped between the microphone and him.

"I just want to ask a few questions." The guy stepped around his dad. "Like why a popular kid would shoot his friends."

"No." His mom shoved Benson and Ryan into their car, while the reporter called out to them. All Benson could do was stare. *A popular kid? Is that all you see?*

"I'm just reporting what everybody wants to know. Like about Steve Ralston." The young guy, doused with the Nikki Harmon syndrome, straightened his button-up shirt. His smirk was eerily like hers. "I'm going to write the book, and you'll want to read it. It's quite a story. About all that's wrong in our schools."

"You're what's wrong," his mom spat, facing the reporter. "Get away from my family," she snarled before she walked around the SUV and got in. "Get us out of here, Tommy."

You think that microphone makes you special? You were one of them, *weren't you?* He could smell the ego, proving Mrs. Matt right about so much.

The hole in his gut forced him to lean his head against the window. *Go away...all of you...just go away.*

Just Monday I told Colin I hated him. He cringed, wishing he could take the words back. But he had learned an important lesson since then. Words caused almost as much pain as guns, and sometimes those who got hurt saw no other out but to use them.

His dad weaved through traffic on the way home, driving almost as erratically as Colin. "You okay, Benson?" His dad glanced too long at him in the rearview, then slammed on his brakes at the stoplight on 47th and Broadway. Ryan whopped him on the arm, like he needed reminding. Chills slithered down his back.

"I'm fine." It was his standby response to everything, thinly veiled for "leave me alone." *Was that how Colin felt, too?*

Benson laid his head back and willed all of it – even the urge to call Colin's cell phone – to go away. With his guard down, he let himself think about Mrs. Matt.

"Help me!" someone had cried. And you just went flying out into the hall to save the day. Why? Why'd you go out there?

"You boys want anything before we head home?" his mom asked as they pulled past their favorite frozen custard place.

"Yeah, just name it. We can stop anywhere." His dad glanced in the rearview.

"I'm pretty whipped, if you don't care. Thanks, though." Benson wanted to smile but just couldn't manage it. His best friend seemed on the same wavelength.

"Think your parents would let you spend the night?" Benson whispered.

"I'd have to call...will they mind?" Ryan pointed at the front seat.

"Mom, can Ryan stay over? There's no school tomorrow." Benson felt slimy using that, but he didn't want to be that alone. They could say a lot without saying a word, and it would feel good to have his best friend to purge with. Even if they did it by playing video games.

"I think that's a great idea," she answered.

Ryan pulled his cell from his back pocket and called home. After begging, he handed the phone over the seat to Benson's mom. "My dad wants to talk to you." After a few minutes, she had assured Mr. Laughlin that his son was in good hands, adding that the camaraderie would be good for both boys.

The minute they got home, Benson and Ryan nabbed a couple of Dr Peppers and headed upstairs. Before they even had a chance to start going over the longest day of their lives, the phone rang. Benson dove across his bed to answer it before his parents could. The boys weren't allowed phone calls after ten, and it was nearly eleven o'clock. Odds were, it was for Colin.

"Benson?" A girl's voice was so quiet, he could barely hear her.

"Yeah?"

Ryan flipped through pages on the bed, but stopped to stare at him to get a signal who it was. Benson's heart hammered hard in his chest.

"Hi, it's Mallorie. I...I just saw your brother here, and he was sure acting strange. Are you coming back tonight?"

He turned sideways, feeling like a mouse sniffing at cheese in the trap. Maybe if he didn't look at Ryan, it wouldn't feel so weird. *Why do I feel so guilty?*

"Uh, not tonight. It's late, and my folks didn't think we should do the all-night thing. We'll be there in the morning, though. What do you mean, *strange?*" He mustered the courage to glance at Ryan over his shoulder, but his best friend had taken intense interest in The Sporting News World Series projections.

"He...he tried to talk to Mr. Barker, but Megan's dad flipped. And then Devin tried to get Colin to leave, but he wouldn't. They're deciding about the whole life support thing tomorrow, and Mr. Barker just told Colin to get out, that nobody wanted to hear his lies. Said he meant it about the police. What does that mean?" She paused, maybe waiting for

Benson to answer, or perhaps trying to think of what to say. "Colin just left, and he seemed pretty upset. What's going on with him, Benson? Why're the Barkers so mad at him?"

Is that what this is? A scoop-digging expedition?

"I'm not sure. But you probably know as much as I do. You're closer connected than I am. Anyway..." Benson kept his back to the room, cringing at the thought of explaining this to Ryan – what a call from the Barbie Brigade would mean to the Operation and to his position on the popularity totem pole. "Maybe I'll see you in the morning."

"Yeah, I'll be here. Let me give you my cell. You got a pen?"

Benson rooted around the junk on his desk for a pen, still keeping his back to Ryan. He felt like a traitor, and he wasn't sure why. But with what she had said about Colin, his heart had stopped fluttering and the whole thing jammed in his throat. *Was Colin about to do something stupid?*

Images of the intersection shimmered through his head. He shuddered.

She gave him the number, adding that she would see him in the morning. He hung up and stared at the seven digits like they were the answer key to every test he'd ever take. Here it was – the first real sign of interest. Mallorie what's-her-name actually knew he existed. But did it matter? After everything that had happened in the past twenty-four hours, to somehow benefit from it made him sick.

He took a deep breath and braced himself for Ryan's twenty questions and maybe a lecture on the perils of swimming in shark-infested waters.

When he turned around, he was shocked and relieved to find his bedroom empty.

"Ryan?" He walked into the hallway, then downstairs to the kitchen. During the entire conversation, he had been stiff with apprehension, worried about Ryan's reaction.

Sitting at the table with a soda and a leftover piece of steak, Colin and Ryan sat discussing the upcoming pennant race. He felt like he'd slipped into an alternate reality.

"When did you get home?" Benson eyed Colin suspiciously, shocked to see him looking almost normal – no more puffy eyes and not appearing nearly as upset as Mallorie made it sound. She said he'd just left and was upset. It fit with the way he drove, but the demeanor didn't.

"Want some?" Ryan asked, motioning for Benson to sit.

Nothing fazes you and that rocks, Benson wanted to say, loving that Ryan would let him off the hook about the phone call. It was what made popular kids crazy when they picked on him.

"Thanks. Is there any more soda?" Benson scrounged through the fridge and found the last Dr Pepper, then plopped across from Colin. "So how'd you get home so fast? One of the girls from the hospital just called and said you were practically in a fight with Mr. Barker."

Ryan jerked his head toward Benson. His eyes said, *For real?* Benson nodded.

"Ah, screw them and the high horse they use for a pedestal." Colin smirked. "Dad says you guys want to go back in the morning. Want me to drive you?" He drained the rest of his Sprite and clanked the can on the table.

"You supposed to be there anymore?" Benson cocked an eyebrow, waiting to read his brother's expression.

"Do I care?" Colin gave another smirk, then ran a hand through his short blond hair, most of it standing up in its wake.

"I guess not. She just said that Mr. Barker ordered you not to come back." Benson popped the tab on his soda, trying to act nonchalant but knowing he danced on thin ice by riling his brother.

"Mr. Barker can kiss my ass. He doesn't own the hospital, and I've got a right to be there. When I'm done, they'll know why." Colin jumped up so fast the oak chair nearly toppled over. He caught it, then made it screech as he shoved it backward. He wadded the paper plate and slammed it into the trash, muttering, "Frickin' idiots got the whole damn thing wrong."

Benson opened his mouth to speak, but what would he say? Colin stomped out of the kitchen and up the stairs.

"Wow...what was *that* all about?" Ryan threw away his

trash while Benson crammed a few chips into his mouth, took a swig of his soda, then let a window-rattling gulp.

"Lifestyles of the bitchy and famous," Benson chimed, one of their age-old responses when describing the stress of being popular.

The two boys trudged upstairs, the comment resurrecting something Mrs. Matt had said. Dating the captain of the football team, or being one, didn't make you cuter or more likely to succeed.

Benson wished he could tell her it must make life harder. Colin was proof of that.

Benson's Journal

Tuesday, Sept. 23rd

Right before Ryan went home to change clothes this morning, I showed him the note and confessed about lying to him. He didn't say much, just read it and said, "Damn" like it really blew his mind. The note, not the lie.

He didn't say a word about me lying, but I could tell it hurt his feelings. He's not all gushy, so he wouldn't say much anyway, but God, I feel like crap.

Colin was already gone when I got up to go pee. No more apologizing for my mouth, I guess, since this journal is for my eyes only from now on. I never thought I'd like writing like this, but it feels good to get stuff out. Mrs. Matt must've known that. Anyway, Colin left before 7 and he's totally not a morning person. He's weirder than ever, not that it'd take much.

Mom and Dad left for work and gave me cash to order a pizza. Mom thinks food can fix everything. Strange thing is, I feel sick to my stomach all the time. Screw eating.

Hope Colin comes back, since he promised to take me and Ryan to the hospital. Though I wouldn't care if he didn't. Don't really want to go there anymore.

Hospitals are about the saddest places ever. But then again, so are schools.

Ryan's Journal

Tuesday, Sept. 23rd

I can't believe Bennie lied to me. I want to be pissed, but then there doesn't seem to be any point. With all that's happened, friendship should be more important than anything. God, I sound like a dang Hallmark commercial.

Colin said some weird crap at the kitchen table last night while Benson was on the phone to his rah-rah girlfriend (okay, it doesn't bother me that a girl likes him, but maybe it burns my rubber a little that she's part of the freakin' Barbie Brigade). Okay, so popular's one thing. It supports the operation, but one of Nikki's friends? Gotta go barf. Be back in 5. I always knew he'd get a girl before me. Dammit. But why couldn't he trust me?

Anyway...Colin said some strange stuff. Here are some samples:

"Did you know steroids make some guys impotent?"

And this one shocked the hell out of me (sorry about the language, Mrs. Ma...whoa, brain lapse. Man, I still can't get used to the idea of you being gone...maybe if I talk to you in here, you won't be really). Okay, so Colin's strangest comment: "I found out that you don't have to wait all that time to get a gun if you go to gun shows. Did you know that?"

I didn't, and I told him so. When I shared that nugget with Benson, he like totally bleached out.

Popular kids sure got a lot of stress. Maybe that's why they throw pharm parties and all that skittling stupidity. Gives new meaning to 'high' school, doesn't it? Just one more reason to infiltrate.

No one else seems to be able to stop them.

Chapter 16

WHEN COLIN FINALLY showed up around nine, Ryan had already walked to their house and eaten a bowl of cereal. Colin burst through the front door, and stared at them – Colinese for *Get your ass moving.*

No one spoke during the drive to the hospital. Benson couldn't tell if times were relapsing to the old *I'd rather beat the snot out of you than be your taxi* mentality. Oddly, when they found a parking place and headed toward the ICU, Colin draped an arm over his shoulder and sighed. "I may need your help after a while, okay?"

Benson nodded, wondering why that made him sick to his stomach. He'd never been his brother's gopher or confidant before, and now seemed like a creepy time to start.

They ran into a group of parents in the hallway between the waiting rooms and asked Mr. Silvey if they could visit Tim. He motioned to his son's door, saying, "He would love to see you two. We'll be in the cafeteria if he needs anything."

Benson and Ryan didn't hesitate. After pushing the heavy door open, Benson peeked around it. He had gotten used to the hospital smell, but he wasn't prepared to see his gothic friend look so fragile ...and normal. Ryan waltzed past Benson, not deterred by the pained expression on Tim's face.

"Hey, freakazoids," Tim muttered, his lips so chapped it seemed hard to talk.

"Hi, stoner. Thought you'd get the front page like all the spotlight hounds?" Ryan grinned, then play-punched Tim's shoulder so gently, Benson wasn't sure he made contact.

"Yeah...that's me...spot...light...hound." Tim took a deep breath. He already seemed tired from the exertion.

"So where'd you get hit? Who shot you? What'd you see?" Ryan dragged a chair closer to Tim's side.

"Ryan, God, give the guy a break." Benson scowled at his best friend – *Dude, he got shot yesterday.* But he knew what Ryan was thinking... in reverse circumstances, Tim would ask the exact same questions.

Tim managed a smile, then slowly replayed what happened to him. He rested periodically, sucked on ice chips, and took ragged breaths that made him twist his face in pain. Benson's head reeled as he listened to a first-hand account of Ralston marching into the office, dragging Megan behind him. In the melee, Steve shot the secretary and four students, Tim getting caught in the line of fire as bullets sprayed through the walls into the conference room where Mr. Drysdale had shoved them. The bullet had been a "through-and-through" in his midsection, rupturing his spleen and wreaking havoc on other organs.

"Damn," Benson mumbled. "Were you in trouble? Is that why you were in the office?"

"Nah...got...nominated for...my charity work." Tim grimaced, then let out a feeble laugh. "Hell, yes, I was in trouble. Trying...to skip. My luck, huh? Bullets are new punishment."

The boys sat and chatted with Tim for a few more minutes, sharing what had happened the rest of the day.

When they finally returned to the waiting room, everyone, including the Barbie Brigade, was somber. Mallorie was lying down across several chairs at the far end of their pow-wow with her face covered by a Britney Spears-type hat – pre-shaven head days. Several parents sat among them now. Makeshift beds had been arranged with chairs pulled together. Pillows and blankets were scattered all along the wall. Benson plopped into a seat in the middle of an empty row within eyeshot of Mallorie and a row from Ryan and the others.

Stuck in the middle.

Pam Utterbeck smirked. "It makes them famous. The shooters, I mean. Eric Harris. Dylan Klebold. That Kip guy and the other one in Paducah. As long as teenagers tease each other, there's gonna be one who goes postal."

"Sad that you know their names," Ryan said. "Hey, Benson, where'd Colin go?"

"Who knows? He's beyond complicated." He scanned the

waiting room where only twenty-five or thirty teenagers remained. Megan Barker's friends didn't seem to have moved, except Mallorie, who kept fidgeting with her blanket and pillow, trying to sleep. Many of the initial crowd hadn't returned yet or maybe didn't intend to.

He suddenly felt slimy being there, like a vulture hovering over road kill. They'd seen Tim, and Benson couldn't help but wonder, what are we waiting for now?

He ached for Mrs. Matt, but he couldn't grieve for her in the hospital. And every time he thought of her, that same rage swelled in his chest, quickly coupled with the suffocating guilt.

Ryan chatted with the rest of the WJHS students about trivial crap, all of them careful to skirt the reason they were there.

Why did I lie to him? He resented that Ryan had gotten past it so quickly, then he felt someone drop into the seat next to him.

"Hi." Mallorie fiddled with the buttons on a royal blue Westwood sweater.

Lisa Kincheloe, Barbie first grade, tossed a black-and-white pebbled composition book next to Mallorie, nearly hitting Benson's leg. "Don't let him see this," Lisa hissed, then sashayed to her pedestal.

"Hey." He stared at the fingers nimbly tracing the button, then let his eyes trail to the composition book, Diva Diary etched in block letters on the front. He wanted to say something profound, to convey how tragic the past twenty hours had been, but he wanted a peek inside that book more.

"Colin was here just a few minutes ago. I saw him outside Megan's room. I can't believe he came back here after last night." Mallorie let go of the Kleenex and finally looked at him. The rest of the Brigade was staring at them. "What did Mr. Barker mean when he said the police would be talking with him, Benson? What did Colin do?"

Benson's heart skipped, then hammered so hard it vibrated in his teeth. He glanced at the composition book again. *Is my name in there?*

"Benson?" She watched his stare and covered the composition book as if he'd seen her underwear.

"Huh? Oh. What'd you say?" His head was reeling. Mallorie was the interrogator, trying to get the 411, and he was the subject.

"Why would Mr. Barker be so angry at Colin?" She scrunched her brow at him, and he wanted to tell her it made her look like she had gas.

"I don't know, Mallorie. I really don't. He's been acting strange since it all started. And I..." But before he could finish, Mallorie tugged his shirt sleeve, then pointed into the hall.

Lurking near a gurney on the opposite side of the corridor, out of sight if Mr. Barker poked his head out of Megan's room, Colin was motioning frantically for Benson.

He reached behind him and smacked Ryan on the arm. "Look!" he ordered, before jogging across the waiting room and into the hall.

Colin yanked him into the enclave outside the men's bathroom. Everyone in the waiting room craned their heads to see. Ryan had followed him halfway across the room but waited and watched like the rest of them.

"Colin?" Benson studied his brother's face. *And I thought you looked normal again?* Colin looked anything but. Gray bags under each eye, a twitch at the edge of his mouth, a permanent frown. His brother was half-past whacked.

The water fountain hummed, someone inside one of the restrooms flushed, and for a split second Benson freaked that it might be Mr. Barker.

"I need you to do me a favor. Take this." Colin's hand trembled as he held out a thin envelope.

"What is it?" Benson took it and turned it over in his hands. He could feel everyone's eyes like lasers on him.

"Don't ask and please don't open it. *Swear* to me you won't." Colin grabbed Benson's arm so hard a sizzle of pain shot through his elbow.

"Ow!" He rubbed his arm, but he nodded. "I swear."

"Okay. Listen, I want you to call Mom and Dad, then get to the police station. Don't let them see that though, okay? You're going to give it to Detective McElhaney. I've talked with him already about some of it, but everything he needs to know is in there. I'm being blamed for something that isn't true, so when you hear it, don't believe it, okay?" Colin's eyes looked like they were filled with red spokes.

Benson had a flashing image of his brother draining a bottle of whiskey, but the notion was too bizarre – wasn't it? A tear spilled over and slid down Colin's cheek.

"Okay," Benson mumbled. What else could he say? He had a hundred questions, but he knew Colin probably wouldn't answer them.

"Please go, okay? Tell Mom and Dad I've gone to the police station to clear up some stuff. Downplay it, Benson. I'm counting on you. Then tell them they need to come pick me up because they're impounding my car to search it. That's when you need to find Detective McElhaney and give him this, okay?"

Benson's head swam, too confused with all the "theys" to sort it out. It was like learning a new game without the rules. He needed to talk to Ryan more than he needed to breathe. "M...Mom and Dad will be at work."

"You're gonna have to call them, Benson. But I need a little time, so spot me twenty minutes." Colin poked his head out and glanced both ways down the hall like he was crossing a street...into the path of a demented Mustang.

"I don't understand. Why're you going?" Benson tried to resist the stares boring into his back. But he couldn't. He glanced over at the teenagers gawking from the waiting room.

"God, it is so messed up. Mr. Barker has, um, assumed some stuff, so if I don't go on my own, they're going to take me in. And I don't want it to go down that way. But I swear to God, Benson, it's not what it looks like."

Take you in?

"God, Colin. I can't stand not knowing. I mean, if you're in trouble...You know Mom and Dad would stop the world from turning to help you."

"There are some things I have to clear up first. Whatever they think in the beginning, I can disprove. That letter is my life, Ben. Don't lose it. Matter of fact, maybe you should make a copy. Ask the nurse where a copier is. Seal the second copy in an envelope and *swear* to me you won't read it. Not yet. Please. I'll let you read it when the time is right. And don't let Mom and Dad see it, for Christ's sake, but get them to the police station by noon. I'm countin' on you, Ben. I gotta jet. You stay true, Ben. Promise." Colin held a clenched fist out, and Benson met it with his own. The gesture felt powerful and made Benson swell with the responsibility.

His brother was gone before he could even stutter.

"I promise," he whispered, caressing the envelope. He turned it over, stared at it, wished for Superman's x-ray vision. *How could I agree not to read it?* It would take tremendous effort and an unfamiliar loyalty to honor it. But he would, because the new bond between them felt good. It felt *right*.

Okay...okay, I can do this... Benson glanced at his watch. It was nearly ten. His mom might be in court, and God only knew where his dad would be. *On a normal day, I'd be in study hall...asking questions, sending preps over the edge...* Benson shivered.

Ryan hurried out into the hall, his eyes wide. "What did he say? What's in the envelope?"

"Yeah, Benson, what's going on?" Nikki Harmon had shoved her way out the waiting room entryway, nearly knocking Ryan over. The rest of the teenagers clamored around him.

"He told me not to believe what I heard at first. None of it is true, he said, and that he could prove it. Gave me this letter to deliver to the police." Benson felt important showing her the letter and felt a twinge of guilt for flaunting it. Mallorie inched closer, staring at the envelope.

"Then let us read it, Benson," Nikki said matter-of-factly.

The sudden spotlight made him nervous. *Colin wouldn't want this...*

"Sorry, ladies. Can't do it." Benson folded the envelope in half. "I made a promise." He tucked it into his back jeans pocket and headed toward the nurses' station. As he turned the corner, Ryan shouted for him to wait up.

"You're such a loser, Benson. You could be part of the crowd." Nikki stood with her hands on her hips, looking like she might run for President if the mood hit her.

"That's just it, Nikki. I *am* part of the crowd. Just not yours."

Pam high-fived another girl, and a few others stifled giggles. Nikki and the other Barbies – minus Mallorie – rolled their eyes and huffed back into the waiting room. Mallorie lingered, smiling at him as he gave her a half-wave.

"Oh, man," Ryan muttered. "Nikki's pissed."

"Like I give a crap," Benson grunted, loud enough for Pam and a few others to hear, then marched to a nurse jotting notes on a metal clipboard. It took nearly five minutes to convince her to copy the letter and give him two envelopes, but with Ryan's help, they got her to do it. He peeled the strips on the adhesive and sealed each before he had a chance to reconsider.

With both letters now stuffed deep into his back pockets, Benson and Ryan caught the elevator.

"What did Colin say?" Ryan asked the instant the door dinged shut. "C'mon, no more holdin' out on me."

Ouch...

"What I told everyone is pretty much what he told me. He said not to believe what I hear. Or something about it not being what it looks like."

"Well, that's cryptic."

They reached the lobby and stood there for a minute. Benson suddenly realized they didn't have a ride. "How're we getting home? I gotta call Mom and Dad. And I have to take *this*..." He pulled one of the envelopes out of his back pocket.

"Let's take a cab," Ryan exclaimed, thrusting the door open. One had just dropped off a fare.

"Do we have enough money?" Benson pulled out his wallet and fingered three crumpled singles.

Ryan produced one, but when they asked the cabbie if they could pay him when they arrived at their house, he agreed.

"What am I gonna say to Mom and Dad? They're going to have a coronary." Benson sat in the backseat and gazed out the window. *How could there be such a beautiful, cloudless day in the midst of all this crap?*

"Well, you need to call them. However Colin explained it,

you need to just tell them. You can't let them find out from the cops. The longer you wait, the harder it'll be."

"He said I had to give him a little lead time. It's only been fifteen minutes..."

"By the time they get the message and call you back, I'm sure he'll have had his cushion. You're stalling." Ryan cocked an eyebrow.

Benson grimaced, then pulled the cell phone from his pocket. While the yellow sedan breezed through traffic, he dialed his mom's office. Relief eased his pounding heart when her voice mail picked up. "Mom, you have to get home as soon as you can, by noon. Me and Colin are okay, but it's, um, sort of an emergency." He flipped the phone closed and repeated the message to his dad's voice mail before he could lose his nerve. "Think they'll freak?"

"Yeah," Ryan said, and grinned. Both their parents were known for certifiable freakage.

When the taxi pulled into his driveway, Benson raced inside to grab the twenty his parents gave him for pizza. After he paid, they foraged in the kitchen and discussed how he was going to explain that Mr. All-America was at the police station. And it wasn't for charity work.

A sliver of unease settled in Benson's stomach. He realized he didn't have a clue why Colin had gone to see that detective. For all his part in the mission, he was nothing but a messenger.

Then why am I scared shitless?

Phone Conversation
Between Benson's Parents

"DID YOU GET a voice mail from Benson? I was in court, and my assistant played it for me in recess." Rebecca Schmidt thumbed through notes in her office while she braced the cell phone between her ear and shoulder.

"Yes, and I don't really have time to break for lunch. Do you want to head home, and I'll try to meet you if I can?" Tommy Schmidt waved to his secretary to check his calendar.

"I think we should both be there. With everything that's gone on...we should be there for Ben. He's gonna have a rough go of it, I think."

"Becca, he's a tough kid."

"That doesn't mean he's not scared. Okay, you're stalling...I'll head home. You get there when you can. But something's not right. I tried to call Colin to see what was going on, but he's not picking up. That's not like him. You call Benson while I head home. I can make my calls from the car."

"I am so damn busy right now. I feel terrible for being annoyed, but I've got appointments all afternoon."

"Tommy, your son's been through a horrible ordeal. Don't forget that."

"I know. It's just insane here right now. I'll call him, and then I'll get there as quick as I can. Maybe I can just postpone everything an hour or so."

By early afternoon, both Schmidts had called their respective secretaries to clear their calendars not only for the day, but the rest of the week.

Chapter 17

BENSON SAT AT the kitchen counter contemplating eating his fifth miniature Snickers. He couldn't decide whether to turn on the tiny kitchen TV. Avoidance had always worked in the past.

Ryan had left twenty minutes earlier, dashing through yards the four blocks to check in with his parents.

Benson heaved a sigh, then punched the power button. Why stop now?

A special bulletin tag ran along the bottom of the screen, but Benson didn't read it. He couldn't stop staring at the jerk reporter, the idiot writer from last night, standing outside Hamilton Memorial Hospital.

"…and the breaking news this morning in Jamestown. Megan Barker died just minutes ago after her life support was turned off. Charges of multiple homicide, upgraded from fourteen to fifteen, have been filed against Westwood freshman Steve Ralston."

The camera focused on a handcuffed Steve, zooming in on his half-sneer as he was led into the police station. His square jaw, dark hair, and dark eyes reminded Benson of an actor, but he couldn't remember the name. *Bad guy from Minority Report?*

But then a flash from grade school sucker-punched Benson.

"No way you're Schmitty's kid brother…you're such a pussy." Steve Ralston gripped Benson by the arms, then shoved him to the ground.

He spit dust, fisted away tears, and tried to get up. Before he managed, a hand grabbed the back of his jeans, jerking him to his feet.

"Red Rover, Red Rover, send the weenie right over!" Ralston sent him flailing toward some other guys who

laughed, then pushed him right back into Steve's arms.

Tears streaked Benson's face, but the shame burned more. Their hands groped him, shoved him from Steve to the other older boys, back and forth, chanting Red Rover.

They laughed, dropped him in the dirt, and pointed at his crotch.

"You frickin' pissed yourself, Shitty Schmitty!" Steve Ralston howled laughter, punching his buddies' arms.

A teacher's whistle sent them running, but their laughter in his head wouldn't go away.

"Losers." Benson stared at the TV, tasting the grit in his mouth from that day in fourth grade. Getting picked on by sixth graders wasn't unique, and he wasn't the only kid Ralston and his thugs bullied.

But Benson could've made it stop. He could've told Colin, a seventh grade god all of Ralston's crew worshipped.

The past slithered away, but the slimy feelings didn't. Watching Steve, feet shackled, scuffle into the precinct sent a surge of satisfaction through Benson. *Yeah, you'll have all kinds of new friends to play Red Rover with where you're going.*

Mr. and Mrs. Ralston hovered just behind their only son, shielding their faces from the glaring spotlight with folders or notepads.

I would too.

Spectators shouted angrily at the family, sporting signs that read, "Commit adult crimes, do adult time," and, "They didn't deserve to die, but you do."

Benson gritted his teeth, the hot sensation filling his chest again. To hell with Red Rover. *You killed Mrs. Matt, you asshole.*

The news continued, some expert analyst giving his prediction about Steve Ralston's defense tactics.

"School shooters are almost always tried as adults. Those Jonesboro boys getting released after just a few years changed that. Michael Carneal is serving twenty-five years, Kip Kinkel got 112, and Luke Woodham got life. Many of them choose to kill themselves. Steve Ralston will undoubtedly plead insanity, and the community will fight his attempt to be tried as a minor."

Benson took a deep breath and tried to put some perspective on what happened.

They're comparing this to Columbine, Paducah, and all those other places...

It made his head swim. The past hours felt like days, weeks even. And now it was going to become a media circus, exactly what Mrs. Matt would've hated.

The reporter thanked the expert, then added an ominous, "But for now, Steve Ralston is in custody, and Westwood Junior High will resume classes next Monday."

The idea made Benson's stomach churn – walking the same halls, wandering into the Media Center to check out books as if he hadn't huddled there fearing for his life.

And the last time I saw Mrs. Matt...

Benson felt the world spiraling out of control – lying to his best friend for the first time ever, his god-like brother at the police station, and the teacher he worked so hard to impress was not going to be at school on Monday. Or ever.

Just before eleven, his dad finally called.

"Benson, what's going on? Don't leave me messages like this." His father was angry, and for a split second, Benson fought the urge to say *never mind* and hang up.

Instead, he blurted, "Colin needs you."

It took Benson ten minutes to convince his dad to get home without breaking his promise to Colin.

Thirty minutes, his dad said, and hung up without saying goodbye. His mom called minutes later – obviously after talking to his dad – and said she was on her way. She said she loved him and not to worry before she hung up, jamming a lump into Benson's throat.

So he'd done his part. His parents were coming home, and he would be able to get them to the police station close to noon. With a little time to burn, Benson hustled upstairs to check his e-mail and IM Ryan. Instead, he froze in front of Colin's closed door.

Do Not Enter, a computerized sign warned. Colin had

laminated it last spring and announced over dinner how serious he felt the sign should be taken. Benson watched his parents exchange one of those looks, then his dad winked at his mom. Nothing they did made sense.

"Colin?" he called, then tapped lightly. He knew the room was empty but counted to ten anyway. He took a deep breath and slowly turned the knob. His nerves jangled as he stood in forbidden territory and surveyed the room. If Colin wanted to hide something, where he would put it? He took two careful steps farther into the room and stopped, inspecting the desk, shelves, TV, stereo.

Benson's heart raced.

I shouldn't be here. He'd beat me like a dog if he saw me in his room. Guilt raced through him, so he turned to leave.

Then he saw it.

The letter jacket. Hanging on the back of the door, the prized possession few sophomores owned. Colin had earned his as a freshman by lettering in basketball and football. His brother seldom left the house without it, regardless of weather. Status was more important than comfort. But Monday had tainted it.

Did Colin know Megan was dead yet? The reporter made it sound like breaking news.

Benson fingered the leather sleeves. Gold material embossed with a sneering yellow jacket under the stitched "Schmidt." Every student at Jamestown High School dreamed of wearing a yellow stinger. Would Benson regret turning his back on a chance to own one? He didn't know, and the fleeting idea of soccer, still a future option, always sat patiently in the back of his mind.

Before he lost his nerve, Benson reached inside each pocket.

Nothing.

Then he opened the jacket and felt for the hidden pockets in the satiny lining. As he slipped his hand deep inside the fabric, his fingers touched several pieces of stiffly wrapped squares. He clasped one and pulled it out.

He stared uncertainly at it for a moment, and then a slew

of emotions shot through him. Without assessing any of them, he straightened the jacket and jetted out of the room. He raced into his own and closed the door quickly behind him. He flipped the lock and sat on the edge of his bed before opening his hand to stare at it again.

Trojan, it read. *Condoms?* Colin had hidden condoms in his letter jacket pocket. Why? Was that why he had to get it from the Barker's house?

His name is on it...

The condoms were either for show, or Megan and Colin had done more than a little casual dating. His brother had always had plenty of girlfriends, but Benson had no idea whether Colin had sex with any of them.

It's not like we were close.

Didn't all the girls joke that they would jump at the chance to make out with someone as "hot" as Colin?

As a seventh grader, Benson imagined making out as copping a feel and *real k*issing. But a girl who dated high school boys played by high school rules, right?

I gotta call Ryan. He didn't do well with secrets, and having a friend like Ryan meant he never had to. He reached for the phone when he heard the front door slam shut.

"BENSON!"

Ah, crap. He tucked the Trojan into his desk drawer under his many treasures and raced down stairs.

"So? Spit it out, Benson. Where's Colin?" His dad stared at him, then thonked the five-hundred dollar briefcase his mom bought last Christmas on the entryway table.

Veins popped in the middle of his dad's forehead, a sign that he was stressed or pissed. Benson didn't like either alternative.

He took a deep breath and muttered, "The police station." He braced for the aftershock.

The veins bulged as his dad loosened one of many Armani ties, and then gave the usual huffing sigh. *C'mon, say something, Dad...*

For ten seconds, his dad stared at him, then finally said, "The police station. Why?"

Before Benson could answer, his mom came barreling though the door. Her harried expression sent his heart trip-hammering again.

They stood frozen in the foyer like going anywhere else might jinx them. Benson's stomach clenched for a minute, panicked that they refused to sit.

This wasn't how it played out in his head. To avoid losing his nerve, he blurted, "Mom, Dad, Colin wanted me to talk to you and explain some things before we go to the police station to get him. I know me and him haven't exactly been close."

His improper use of grammar would normally have evoked a correction from his mother, but both his parents were obviously too tense to notice. Benson gathered his thoughts and continued.

"Colin has been dating Megan Barker for a couple of months now. They'd gotten really serious, and Steve Ralston was totally bent because of it. He even threatened to murk him, not that Colin thought he really meant it, but..."

"Murk him?" His mom shook her head like he was speaking Chinese.

"Oh, uh, hurt him, maybe even kill him. But who would've thought Steve really meant it?" Benson took a deep breath and continued. "Colin said there was some stuff he needed to explain to the police and to you. Mr. Barker is *so* ticked off, I think because he found out Colin slept with his daughter. So now Colin's gone downtown to answer some questions, and..."

"WHAT?" his father shouted, lurching toward Benson, ready to rattle someone's cage. Benson preferred it not be his. "Why the hell would he do such a stupid...?"

"Dad, let me finish. Please."

It was the first time he'd ever felt like a man speaking to his father. And his dad listened, leaning back against the foyer table, motioning for Benson to hurry up.

"Colin told me to get you to the police station by noon. He apparently has information for this detective and didn't seem scared about going to the police, because he knows he hasn't done anything wrong. He wanted you to know that right up front."

His mom started to pace. She grumbled something, but Benson couldn't make out the words. He had a fleeting thought about Megan being only fourteen and he'd seen all kinds of stuff on TV about sex with girls that age.

"We need to go. Is that all, Benson?" His father's face had gone from the waning summer tan to Coca-Cola red.

They all looked at the grandfather clock at the same time. It was 11:50. It would take at least fifteen minutes to get there, especially through lunch traffic.

"Dad, Colin called your lawyer. Uh, because of stuff about Steve. And...and he *really* wanted me to make sure you understand that what you hear at first *is not true*." He placed the same emphasis on those words that Colin had.

"What the hell does *that* mean?" his mother snapped.

"I don't know, Mom. I tried to ask, but he wouldn't tell me." Benson made no mention of the letter. He had made Colin a promise.

"Let's go." His father demanded, furious and ready to take it out on someone.

God, I never wanna piss him off like this.

His mom had composed herself and was back in attorney mode. Benson wondered how the family lawyer would ever form his own opinions with Rebecca Schmidt bending his ear. Even though she didn't practice criminal law, it wouldn't stop her from giving her two cents' worth.

And Benson put his money on it being heftier than a couple of pennies.

His parents marched out the door, nearly plowing over Ryan, who was sitting on the front porch. Neither said a word as Ryan joined them, too much part of the family for them to notice or care.

As the two boys slid into the backseat, Benson's stomach fluttered. He suddenly felt six again and on the verge of tears. He recalled a time he confessed to swiping a fishing lure from Jed's Farm and Home. He felt the same pressure as the questions started.

"Why didn't he tell us about her?" His mother's pursed lips were almost white.

"I'm not sure. Maybe because he was dating a girl at my school. Maybe that's why he told me." With that realization, Benson felt the first inkling of pride. And something else he couldn't quite pinpoint.

"How do you know Megan died?" His dad looked at him in the rearview. Ryan jerked sideways, the information obviously news to him.

"I saw it on the news. But I bet Colin doesn't know." Benson shivered. He couldn't imagine Colin's reaction.

"Oh, I'm sure the police will make a *point* of letting him know," his mom said.

"What does Colin have on Ralston, Benson?" His dad barely slowed at a stop sign, whipping left and sending both boys sliding to the right.

"He didn't say." Benson righted himself, then carefully pulled one of the envelopes from his back pocket and held it down low. He'd forgotten to put one of them in his lockbox. The desire to peek now was overwhelming.

Ryan raised his eyebrows and nodded, mental for *Man, let's read it.*

"Well, what else *did* he say?" His mom's irritated tone scared Benson a little. When she got mad, the boys had always known to skirt her.

"Did you boys break my lamp?" Mom's hands were on her hips, and she had the scowl that put the deep wrinkle between her eyes. "Colin? Benson?"

Four-year-old Benson hid behind his big brother.

"Nuh-uh, Mommy, the Boogie Man did it...he was chasing us. For real." Colin gave that deep-dimpled smile that always made people squeeze his cheeks, but Mommy's frown just got bigger.

"When you're ready to tell the truth, young man, you can come out of your room. Go! Now!" Her tone was harsh and made Benson have to hold his privates.

Sitting in the backseat, he remembered that fear well. His mom had never once spanked either of them, but her anger and disappointment ranked right up there with lima beans.

"Benson!" she snapped.

"Huh?"

"What else did Colin say? We can't go in there without all the details." She sighed, more ticked than ever that she couldn't stop the Earth's rotation.

"He talked about Megan, but that's all." He could see the police station just past the stoplight and couldn't have been more relieved. His parents were wound up tight, and he pitied anyone who got in their way.

"I hope they have more answers than you do," his dad said with a grunt. He parked in a handicapped space and was halfway to the door before Benson and Ryan were able to get out of the SUV.

"Why's he so mad at you?" Ryan slammed the door.

"Who else is he gonna take it out on?" Benson hung back. "Wait up. I gotta get this to Detective McElhaney, remember? I can't do that with Mom and Dad around."

They let his parents enter the precinct, then went to the large desk at the front of the main lobby.

"I, uh, need to speak with Detective McElhaney," Benson said, then looked around to make sure his parents were out of earshot. Ryan stood right behind him, either to have his back or to hide, Benson wasn't sure which.

The large room behind the desk was a swirl of activity. Phones rang, people waited in chairs while others sat next to desks being asked questions. His parents were shaking hands with a man in a wrinkled suit. The chaos made it hard for Benson to focus.

"Sure, kid. And I gotta see Angelina Jolie." The bearded officer chuckled, then coughed until he took a swig of something from a giant convenience store cup.

Benson frowned. "I've got something really important for him. It's about the Steve Ralston case. It's from Colin Schmidt."

The officer raised his bushy eyebrows. "I'll just take it for you, son," he said, and reached for the letter.

"No," Benson snipped, jerking the envelope back and hugging it to his chest like a treasured baseball card.

A woman near the back of the room shrieked, "You better

arrest my husband or I'm gonna kill him!"

Benson flinched. He suddenly felt like he was back in the Media Center, cowering as he listened to screaming in the hall.

Ryan sensed his best friend's discomfort. "C'mon, Ben. I bet he's upstairs. That's where your parents headed."

"Hang on, squirt. Nobody's goin' nowhere." Sergeant Preston, according to his name badge, seemed perplexed by the teenager's insistence. Without taking his eyes off Benson, he picked up the telephone and made a curt request for McElhaney. He explained what the kid had for the detective, then raised his dark thick eyebrows again. He slammed the phone in its cradle.

"You better not be yankin' my chain here, kid. Detective McElhaney will be right here. Seemed pretty excited about that letter."

The sergeant directed the two boys to sit on the bench under the window. Only four minutes passed before an enormous lumberjack of a man loomed before the two seventh graders.

Sergeant Preston grunted. "You boys're on the A list today. Detective McElhaney doesn't hurry for anybody."

Chapter 18

STARING AT THE massive man behind the desk, Benson tried to keep his bobbing knee still. The office was cramped, stacked files everywhere, and not an inch of the metal desk was showing. Three wanted posters on a bulletin board drew his attention, and when the man finally spoke, Benson's knee did double-time.

"Did you read this letter, boys?" Detective Patrick McElhaney stared at them with an odd smile and a cocked eyebrow.

"No, sir." Benson shook his head too hard. His hands trembled as he stared at the detective. *He doesn't believe us.*

"C'mon, boys, you had a letter that had answers to the school shooting and maybe other juicy tidbits...and *you didn't read it?*" Detective McElhaney's expression didn't change. He looked from Benson to Ryan and then settled his gaze back on Benson.

"Well, it doesn't matter anyway. I don't suppose you had anything to do with *this* anonymous note, did you?" McElhaney stared deep into Benson's eyes.

"What anonymous note?" Benson, truly caught off guard, glanced at Ryan. "We didn't write any note. Why would we?"

"I don't know. Why would you? Some fellow Westwood classmates have made a serious claim about Steve Ralston..." Detective McElhaney said, holding up a single typed page. The letter was too far away to read, but Benson's wild-eyed expression had to support his claim.

"Sir, I've never seen that. Can't you like run prints on it? Find what kind of paper it was printed on? Something?" Benson's heart raced. *Who would write an anonymous note? It wasn't Colin, obviously, so who else?*

Detective McElhaney chuckled. "You watch too much CSI,

son. Now about this other letter. Your friends know you have it?"

"Well, yes, sir. They were watching when Colin gave it to me." Benson's knee hopped to duty again.

"Hmmm. Okay, thanks, boys. I'll be in touch if I need anything." Detective McElhaney picked up a file, opened it, and put his glasses back on. Just like that, Benson and Ryan were dismissed.

"But..." Benson scooted to the edge of his seat.

"But what?" The detective's stare burned into him. "I've got work to do, and unless you have new information..."

Benson thought for a moment – flashes of the letter jacket, the condom, Colin insisting things weren't what they appeared. But he said nothing.

Detective McElhaney's eyes narrowed slightly. "You boys go on upstairs, next floor up. Colin's in an interview room up there. I'll be in touch if I need anything, okay?"

"Okay," Benson agreed. Ryan was already halfway out the door.

I have information for you, Benson wanted to add, having a sudden revelation as he closed the door behind him. *Our Operation Cappuccino caused this whole mess.*

He didn't know if he really believed that any more, but the hollowness in the pit of his stomach served as a constant reminder of the possibility.

Being in a police station somehow magnified his guilt.

When they made their way upstairs, discussing who they thought wrote the anonymous note and what it said, they saw his parents sitting in a waiting area talking to Philip Traynor, their lawyer and close family friend. The boys kept their distance, sitting twenty feet away on a bench next to another interrogation room.

"Why're we here, Benson?" Ryan whispered. "Let's go outside and wait. This place creeps me out."

Before Benson could answer, his mom barked, "Philip, I want to know where Colin is – now. I want to be in there, do you hear me?" She stalked to one of the interrogation rooms and yanked the door open. Peering inside and obviously seeing no one, she slammed it shut.

His dad paced, pausing long enough to peer through another interrogation door's pebbled glass. Benson had never seen his dad so flustered. "Is he under arrest? And what is all this about the hospital? That man is accusing Colin of..."

"Tommy, slow down. Colin came here willingly. They're finding out which room he's in now, and I know they're stalling, but Colin's not in any trouble...yet." Mr. Traynor set his briefcase down in an empty seat and straightened his tie.

"Well, go find out, Phil. I don't want Colin questioned without you – or me. I'll slap a lawsuit on them so fast their heads will implode." His mom, sounding more like an attorney than a mother, had her arms folded across her chest like she meant to ground everyone in the precinct.

"I'm sorry he asked to speak to me first...but you know I've got to honor him as a client. I hope you understand." Mr. Traynor stood facing his dad, so Benson couldn't hear the muffled response.

His mom, however, made no effort to keep her voice down. "Just find him, Phil. Why're you just standing here?" Her voice cracked – beyond pissed.

"Why did Colin ask to see him first?" Ryan whispered.

"I don't know. Maybe we should read the letter." Benson shifted to feel the remaining envelope in his pocket. He watched Mr. Traynor beat a path back and forth on the walkway that surrounded all the desks in the middle. Officers on the phone, some questioning people and scratching away on clipboarded forms, a few one-finger tapping on computers. Phones rang non-stop, and each person Mr. Traynor stopped and talked to pointed toward someone else.

Philip Traynor finally got angry and stomped downstairs.

"Does that mean he can't find Colin?" Ryan glanced over at Benson's parents.

"God, that's not good." Benson watched his mom and dad and wondered what they would say to Colin. Would their perfect son finally disappoint them?

Contrary to what he would've thought, the idea made Benson's stomach hurt.

Interview Notes
With Colin Schmidt

Subject: Colin Thomas Schmidt, 16, September 23rd
NOTE: videotaped interview
Interviewer: Detective Scottie Pembleton (DP) and Detective Randolph Barnes (DB)
Transcribed notes from videotaped interview; Transcriber: Sarah Graham, Jamestown PD
TRANSCRIBED INTERVIEW:

DB: *So you raped her?*

CS: *I didn't rape her.* (Note: CS's face flushed, balled fists.)

DB: *Your girlfriend was three months pregnant, wiseass. Doctors didn't know in time to save the baby. With blows sustained to her abdomen, the fetus probably died not long after the attack. Why didn't you tell us?*

CS: *I don't have to put up with this crap. I know my rights.*

Note: CS crosses arms across chest, serious attitude.

DB: *Why're you so pissed off if you haven't done anything wrong?*

CS: *Because you're a jerk. I know what you're doing... trying to rile me about Megan, and...* (Note: CS unable to finish, crying)

DB: *And?*

CS: *And I didn't make Steve Ralston shoot all those people. Ralston's juiced. If you were out there doing your job, you'd know that.*

DP: *But you knew she was pregnant?*

CS: *I just found out last weekend. Megan did a home pregnancy test. We talked about what we should do. She was real scared.* (Note: CS's hands trembling significantly, crying a lot).

DP: *And now she's dead. How does that make you feel, Colin?*

CS: (Long pause) *How do you think?* (Note: CS crying)

DB (grabs subject's shirt): *You little prick, you slept with her! Ralston saw his girl in your letter jacket and ran home to get his daddy's guns. He came back and killed 15 people!*

CS: *I didn't put that gun in his hands or pull the trigger! I didn't make him take steroids! I didn't piss in his Cheerios!*

DB: *You think you're some hot-shit Mr. All-America. Just because Daddy's got money and your name is in the paper every weekend. It don't mean nothin', kid. I don't care who you are. You got that girl pregnant, and she's only 14. That's statutory rape any way you crack it up.*

Note: Attorney Philip Traynor interrupts interrogation, accuses detectives of unauthorized interrogation.

PT: *Are you badgering my client, Detective? Is this boy under arrest? Has he been advised of his rights? I've been trying to find him for twenty minutes while I was given the runaround, and I guarantee Rebecca Schmidt will slap a lawsuit on your ass for this.*

DB: *Rebecca Schmidt's son is here of his own free will, Mr. Traynor.*

PT: *Don't say another word, Colin. I'll take it from here.*

Note: CS bursts into tears, PT whispers in client's ear, inaudible.

DP: *He's not under arrest, Traynor, don't get your panties in a bunch. I have it all on tape. Ask him.*

PT: *This boy is 16 years old, Detectives. He asked for his lawyer on the phone over an hour ago, and I have THAT on tape. Anything you got is inadmissible, and you know it. I don't care what Mike Barker said Colin did, it's hearsay. His mother is the assistant district attorney, and I'd say you just bought your little department a judicial nightmare.*

DP: *Knock yourself out, Traynor, we're done with the little rapist – for now.*

Note: PT and CS spend 43 minutes talking, no audio per attorney request. PT escorts CS out of interrogation room at 1:52 p.m.

Ralston Conference in Interrogation II

THE FOLLOWING INTERVIEW was tape-recorded by Bryant Emery, III, LLC, as requested by Robert Ralston, II, and approved by the family's retained attorney, Alex Sheffield. Transcribed by personal assistant Mickaela Blankenship.

Tuesday, September 23 12:45 p.m.
Interrogation Room II: Robert Ralston in an observed interview with his son, Steven Ralston.
RR: *"They're transporting you to Havenwood, son. Your mother has run to the house to get you a few things. They said you could have a notebook, your Ipod, and a few clothes, so your mom's going to meet us there with your stuff. I can't drive you since...since you're in police custody. Why haven't you changed clothes? Didn't they want these?"*
SR: *"They took my over shirt, said they would take the rest when I got booked. This embarrass you? Me in bloody clothes? This is only the beginning, Dad. Only the beginning."*
RR: *"If you're going to be an ass, I'm leaving. Otherwise, they said I could ride with you. Are you okay with that?"*
SR: *"I don't give a shit what you do. Suit yourself."*
RR: *"This is going to be hard for us too, Steve, but you have to own up now." [long pause] "Maybe Havenwood will help."*
SR: *"A shrink isn't going to fix me."*
RR: *"There's not going to be any bail, you know that. People in this town are liable to lynch you if they see you. Havenwood's an hour and a half away, so it'll give you breathing room. We'll be able to come see you on weekends. Next Tuesday we meet with the DA. We'll plea bargain and*

deal this thing out. You'll get less time that way and save yourself the embarrassment of a messy trial."

SR: "Save **me** the embarrassment? Get real, Dad." [SR laughs] "Yep, a messy trial might embarrass the crap outta me."

RR: "Shut up, Steven, just shut up."

SR: "Yes, sir." [SR salutes. RR raises a hand]

BE: "Robert, no."

RR: "You know, son, I'd like to be able to discuss this with you like a man. The fact is, you're right. You've ruined everything, and I don't get it." [Long pause] "Frankly, Steven, I'm having a hard time looking you in the face right now."

SR: "Who cares? I deserve what I get. But that slut won't..."

BE: "STEVE! Nothing incriminating that I shouldn't hear."

SR: "Then leave."[Long pause] "She got hers, that's all. And that prick ain't taking what don't belong to him. If he'd answered his damn cell phone, it would've been a perfect day."

RR: "I can't imagine you really think that. What would make you do this, Steve? Help me understand."

[SR laughs] "You will never understand. You were Mr. Yellow Jacket. Everything in your life has been perfect. Until now."

RR: "Surely you didn't think I could fix this. I can't. [Long pause] When we walk out of here, don't answer any of the questions they're going to throw at you. The TV stations will twist everything, so you gotta keep your mouth shut. Even if some of your friends try to call or come see you. Nothing. Do you hear me?"

SR: "Who the hell would come see me, Dad? [smirks] Maybe that idiot Benson knew something I didn't."

RR: "Who? And don't get cross with me, Steve. I'm sure you've thought of calling someone, maybe Carter or Brendon. But they're not going to want to see you right now – maybe not ever. I've spent these last few days trying to understand what you've done. You're my son, and I love you. But this...

this...I can't even process it. What's happened to you?"

SR: [turned to BE] *"Can I answer that?"*

BE: *"No."*

RR: *"I just don't know how you go from being an All-American athlete with everything, and now every single person in Jamestown hates you...us. Our whole family is going to have to deal with this now. It's no longer just about you, Steve, so think about the plea bargain Mr. Emery discussed."*

SR: *"I don't want a plea bargain, Dad. Diminished capacity, that's what Alex said earlier. Some new rage or Twinkie defense he's come up with. And then we'll move when...if...I'm acquitted."*

RR: *"Steve, without a plea bargain, you'll get life in prison, period. What do you think is going to get you a rage defense? Why would you risk that?*

SR: *"Oh, there are things...you didn't know everything about me, Dad, believe it or not. You think these muscles come easy?" [SR flexes right bicep]*

RR: *"I don't even know you. [Long pause] Spend some time thinking hard about what you want. Remember that a plea bargain could mean a few years in Havenwood, then maybe a few in prison. You might be out by your thirtieth birthday."*

SR: *"We have people like Alex Sheffield on the payroll for a reason. I can't do time, Dad. You don't get it. This was supposed to be final, ya know? I just can't..."*

RR: *"What did you just say?"*

SR: *"Ah, never mind. You wouldn't understand."*

[Two officers enter the room] "Time to go."

[Due to shoulder injury, SR's hands are front-cuffed, ankles shackled, and suspect is led from interrogation room II.]

Chapter 19

WHEN PHILIP TRAYNOR emerged from the interrogation room down the hall, Benson leapt to his feet.

Oh, my God...

Colin walked out behind Mr. Traynor, shoulders slumped and his head down. He looked thirty, and let out a ragged sigh that sounded just as old. If Benson didn't know any better, he'd swear Colin had entered a time warp. Both their parents rushed him, wrapping their arms around him.

His mom held him at arms length, brushing the clumped hair from his eyes. "Oh, son, why'd you agree to talk with them on your own? Didn't you trust us?" His mom's eyes filled with tears and some weird expression Benson had never seen.

Colin, obviously unable to talk, couldn't stop his chin from trembling. Benson's heart tugged, his throat too sticky to speak. He fought the urge to run.

"Son, you could've talked to us about all this. You didn't have to call Philip." His dad put an arm around Colin and turned to head Benson and Ryan's way.

"I'm really tired. Can we go home? Benson delivered a letter that explains all of this." Colin looked up and met Benson's gaze.

Benson nodded, swelling with pride.

Colin let out a ragged sigh, maybe closer to forty now. "I...I told Mr. Traynor everything, but I just can't talk about it anymore..." His shoulders drooped, and both parents exchanged a glance over their son.

Benson watched the worry crease both their foreheads and then raised his eyebrows at Ryan. His best friend shrugged. They wandered over to the adults, hanging back, trying to be wallpaper.

I've done it for years...just not like this.

"Can we take him?" His dad turned to Mr. Traynor, then looked around to see if a detective intended to talk with them.

"Yes, they're letting you take him home...for now. I think I'll join you for a drink in your den, if that sounds okay." Traynor's business tone told the two Schmidts – and Benson – that the information would come then, not in the precinct.

"That sounds great, Phil. We'll meet you there. So that's it? All this to-do, and now they're just done with him?" His dad wiped a bead of sweat from his forehead.

Had his dad ever sweated like that? It was hot out, but not in the precinct. Seeing his parents so nervous scared him.

"The police are going to want to talk to him again, but they'll do it through me. There are, um, situations I need to discuss with you. But not here."

"They may be finished with us, but I'm not finished with them," their mom snipped. And Benson could tell from her tone that someone would pay for her frustration.

The four of them stood in the middle of the hallway between Interrogation Room I and II when Benson realized everyone in the precinct was staring at them. He could feel sets of eyes studying them, judging them. Several officers at their desks turned to gawk.

Not quite the same headlines we're used to: Golden Boy questioned, career down the toilet. See page 2 for story. Benson shivered.

"Phil, we'll meet you at the house. Boys..." Benson's dad nodded to Ryan and him. "Why don't you two ride with Mr. Traynor, okay? We need to talk to Colin on the way home."

Whether he wants to or not...

Before Benson could answer, Colin turned and squeezed his shoulder. "Hey, Ben, thanks. For everything."

Benson blushed. "No problem."

Colin nodded, and the two brothers bumped fists. A surge of pride flooded Benson. It was a feeling he was getting used to, and one he liked.

"We need to go," his dad said, nudging Colin forward. Without saying anything else, they left the precinct and trudged outside. Before Benson was even aware of them, a sea of reporters pounced. Clicking cameras, microphones shoved in front of them, and a wall of faces. Angry questions ignited.

"Colin, have you been arrested?" one shouted.

"What role did you have in the shooting?"

"Were you and Steve Ralston friends?"

"Where were you when..."

Philip Traynor pulled Colin back inside the precinct's lobby. The Schmidts, Ryan included, clamored behind them and shut the door on the hungry wolves. "Damn," his dad muttered.

"Let's go out the back." Philip motioned to an officer at a desk, the sergeant who had given Benson and Ryan a hard time about delivering their letter. *Guess he knows not to underestimate kids anymore.*

A door clicked open to the left of the desk, and Ryan mumbled, "Feels like an episode of *Law & Order.*"

When they emerged into a parking garage full of police cars, cages, and officers streaming in and out of the building, Benson let out his breath. No reporters, no cameras, no shouting. He was tired of shouting.

He looked around for daylight, for the exit. He was ready to be outside, with sun streaming on his face so he could forget all the sadness of the past few days.

"You all wait here. I'll get my SUV and drive you around to your car," Philip said. He headed toward a walkway that led into the sunlight Benson craved.

When Mr. Traynor disappeared, Colin shuffled his feet and mumbled, "Mom, Dad, I...I'm really sorry about all this..."

His dad gave Colin's shoulder a squeeze while his mom stood on the other side of him. Benson and Ryan drifted a few steps back. Hearing Colin grovel made Benson squeamish.

"I never knew this was back here," Ryan said, as they studied the garage. "This is cool."

"Really, Mom, I know you're mad, but..." Just as Colin started to purge his guilt, to maybe spill his guts about everything – *the condom even?* – Benson heard a ruckus. Officers opening the back door of a police car, one standing with his feet apart and talking into a radio. Then two men flanked a teenager being escorted out another back door of the police department, less than twenty feet from where Benson stood.

When he understood what he was seeing, his mouth fell open. Colin's words broke off mid-sentence, hovering in the air like an escaped balloon.

All the sounds of the afternoon seemed to suddenly fade. Benson's back-and-forth gaze volleyed from his brother's wide-eyed, jaw-dropped expression to the slumped figure across the parking garage – Jamestown's most hated resident.

Steve Ralston, head so low his chin nearly touched his chest, trailed behind a team of expensive suits coming out of the police station. *Right next to the same door we just came out of...*

No matter how muggy it was, Benson shuddered. Time jellied as he stared at Ralston. The idiot looked like a death row inmate being led to the electric chair. Hands cuffed in front of him, he shuffled his feet, letting his Tommy jeans drag the floor. A white tee shirt outlined a man's muscular body, but his stature contradicted it.

Benson watched Colin's jaw clench. Splotches of red spotted his cheeks and neck, and sweat popped out on his forehead. For that brief instant, Benson had a surge of telepathic energy from his brother – *I WISH YOU WERE DEAD!*

Colin couldn't tear his eyes off Ralston, and the fire in his glare must have crossed the twenty feet of concrete, because Steve turned and looked up. A maniacal grin spread across Ralston's face, his eyes so wild, he barely resembled the boy Benson had interviewed only a week earlier.

Or the one on the playground...

Colin and Ralston had even played Mighty together. The images were ludicrous, like dancing clowns at a funeral. Steve playing football, Red Rover, then toting guns – it garbled Benson's brain. He didn't need another flash of telepathy to know what Colin was about to do. It was written all over his brother's face.

Colin spun away from his parents too fast for anyone to react. And nothing any of them could have done would've been fast enough anyway.

Chapter 20

BENSON HAD A fleeting image of interviewing Steve and wincing at the put-down, *"How could someone have such a cool brother and be such a damn geek?"* The memory made him shiver, but before he could assess the eeriness, Ralston uncorked and the garage erupted.

Steve head-butted the officer who stood between him and Colin – or freedom. Blood sprayed from the cop's nose and voices screamed, "TASER HIM!"

Another shouted for a gun as Steve flung his cuffed hands like a crazed lunatic. He whacked one cop, slammed into a second, and just like that, Steve Ralston had broken free.

The cops bringing him out weren't armed? Are you kidding me?

Benson's stomach iced in panic. He scrambled backward a few steps, his parents yelled for him to get down, Ryan grabbed at him, but Benson couldn't stop staring at Ralston. That same syrupy sense of time from the Media Center made the whole thing too slow, too real, too much like yesterday.

Cops scrambled for Steve, but he whaled his cuffed hands at the officers, popped one in the mouth, another in the side of the head, and then kneed a third in the groin. He swung his arms in one all-out blow and had separation. Cops shouted at him, a pulse of furious panic spiraling throughout the garage.

"Grab him!" one officer shouted, and another bellowed, "Taser him!"

"Screw that! Shoot him!" the guy with the bloody nose screamed in rage.

A pair of unsuspecting cops coming out of the building never saw Ralston coming. He plowed through them, all three grunting with the impact.

Game saving tackle! roared through Benson's head, the

same announcer from his 47th and Broadway dream. *I'm losing it...*

"Benson! Ryan! Get over here!" His mom waved frantically for the boys to get their butts behind a black-and-white Jamestown patrol car. It seemed too surreal to be happening, and Benson froze, the image of Mrs. Matt stooped behind the Media Center doors overlapping with Steve yanking at one of the downed officer's belt. The second patrolman scrambled after Ralston, shouted for him to stop. But Steve already had his partner's Glock, and smacked him brutally upside the head, hard enough to knock him out. In a strangely fluid maneuver, Steve rolled over both unconscious officers, using them as a shield, then dashed behind a concrete support. Random gunfire peppered the wall and beam only inches from where Steve hid.

Bullets pinged metal, heads dropped behind cars, and cops roared for armed officers to open fire.

This can't be happening...no...

Benson clamped his hands over his ears, but he had to watch...

Steve's head emerged, then ducked behind the concrete beam. Ryan yanked at the back of Benson's shirt so hard it pulled him to his butt with an excruciating jolt to his tailbone.

"Ah, God!" Benson screamed, then scooted until he felt his dad's strong arms around his chest tugging him backward.

"Put your guns down! NOW! Or I'll do it!" Steve screamed, then emerged with the barrel of the pistol shoved under his own chin. Four or five cops hovering behind vehicles had their guns leveled on Steve, and Benson couldn't imagine why they weren't firing.

Go ahead! Shoot him! Who cares if he blows his brains out! Benson trembled with the same fear and pulsing adrenaline he'd experienced only a day earlier.

Cops shouted orders, guns ready to lay Ralston out, but a radio crackled for them to control the situation. "Don't fire!" a frantic voice yelled. "DO *NOT* FIRE!"

What the hell's wrong with you people! SHOOT HIM! Benson's blood burned with fury that they gave a crap about

Steve Ralston's life after all he'd done. Steve took careful sidesteps, inching toward a patrol car only two spaces from where Benson and his family crouched. Colin's eyes were glassy. *With panic? Hatred?* As Benson waited, his whole body trembled. Colin's steady hands gripped the bumper of the patrol car.

No, Colin... Benson sensed his brother's urge to jet after Steve.

"I'll do it, I swear. GET BACK!" Steve shoved the gun harder into the soft flesh under his chin, his erratic gestures making officers twitch, except Mr. Ralston, who screamed at Steve to put the gun down. He marched right toward his son with officers ordering him to get back, get down, get out of the way. But he didn't. He closed the distance and reached for Steve's gun hand.

An inch from having the pistol, his dad gave Steve the perfect barrier. Even Benson could see that. With the human blockade, Steve dropped and rolled behind the nearest police car. Someone fired, and fury pulsed in the parking garage.

"There's a civilian in the line of fire! *STOP!*"

For a few moments of menacing silence, no one moved. Déjà vu overwhelmed Benson, threatened to sideline him for the duration when all he could smell for a split second was the urine and vomit from the Media Center.

Ryan hissed, "Look!"

Benson focused on Ryan's pointing finger and saw officers signaling to one another and maneuvering around the garage. He could no longer see Steve or Mr. Ralston. But when Ryan motioned frantically at the foot of space underneath their black-and-white, both boys dropped to their bellies to look. A zing of fear shot through Benson when he saw the Tommy jeans dragging the concrete on the other side of their car.

Oh, God... The thought had barely finished when he jolted upright and saw Colin near the rear of the car, neck craning to see behind it. Their dad jerked Colin's shirt, but the fabric ripped, and he yanked himself free, his bright red face bizarrely catatonic.

"Colin!" his mom screamed.

In a flurry of scrambling feet and a strange quarterback sneak, Colin launched himself from behind the car. Benson jumped up, trying to see.

"'Bout time, prick," Ralston seethed.

"You killed her!" Colin growled, and the unmistakable sound of bodies slamming to pavement followed.

"No, asshole, you did! You made me do it!"

Panic sliced through Benson's insides. Officers clamored toward the boys just as the first shot exploded.

"Don't shoot!" cops yelled. "There's another kid!"

Benson's mom howled, his dad trying to get out of her clutching grasp.

Mr. Ralston screamed, "Don't shoot my son!"

Gunfire erupted like a gross of firecrackers all lit at once. The smoke burned Benson's nostrils, but he vaulted around the car. An officer tried to shove him back.

What he saw would burn in his memory for the rest of his life. But Benson didn't focus on Colin's still body beneath Steve Ralston, still staring – no, *smiling* – down at his brother.

"GET OFF HIM!" Benson screamed, and Steve raised his wobbling head, blood streaming down the side of his face. An officer barked at Steve to put the gun down, for Benson to get out of the way, for everyone to shut the hell up.

Benson couldn't think with all the yelling, couldn't breathe when he locked eyes with Ralston, now covered with his brother's blood. Without hesitation – no longer just a spectator – he lurched at Steve and swung with all his might. He landed a solid punch on Steve's jaw, his knuckles crunching excruciatingly against Ralston's jaw. He was thrown aside a split second later. When he looked up, Steve sneered, then raised the gun slowly, deliberately, the barrel aimed at Benson's chest.

Oh, God...

The explosion of gunfire was deafening, but the sight of Steve's jerking body sent a surge of vicious victory roaring through him.

Chapter 21

THE ECHOING DEMANDS and barrage of orders made no sense to Benson as he lay on his back, trying to raise himself to his elbows. He stared at the bloody image of Steve Ralston lying on top of his brother. Officers stooped beside them, pressing forefingers to each teenager's neck.

"Cuff that kid!"

"I've got a pulse! Medic!"

"Get him off...and..."

"I REPEAT, OFFICER DOWN!"

"We need a bus. NOW!"

It sounded like a confused foreign language. An officer grabbed Benson, threw him over onto his stomach, and slapped cold metal cuffs on his wrists, cinching them so tight it pinched his skin.

"Get those off him!" Philip Traynor boomed as he came running past the wall of officers blockading people, yellow tape already being wrapped around support beams.

Heated exchanges, frantic officers dragging Steve's motionless body clear of the car. Another cop peeled his mother from Colin, snapping that they had to get him to the hospital. Someone started giving him CPR, feet pounded the pavement from all directions, people screamed, gawkers tried to get a look. *Get away from us!*

For several agonizing minutes, Benson's entire body trembled. Tears spilled down his cheeks as a cop got bloody performing mouth-to-mouth on his brother. When the officer paused to answer a question, Colin's head lolled toward Benson, eyes staring but unseeing.

Why did you do this, Colin? WHY?

His mom grappled with the man to let her hold her son, his father trying to keep her out of the way. Ryan turned to him, said something, but no matter how much their mouths moved, Benson's world had gone silent.

An eternity later, an ambulance backed into the garage and Colin was lifted into it. Both his parents dove into the back, and his family was whisked away without saying a word to him.

"I'll get you there, boys," Philip Traynor assured him.

Mr. Ralston bellowed that they had killed his son.

Someone pressed fingers into Steve's neck and mumbled, "He's gone."

Benson was hefted to his feet. The cuffs were removed, but he didn't care. All the commotion roared through his brain, his ears ringing with the gunfire, the explosions that had whizzed inches by him.

The cop Steve had clubbed on the head was being helped into a patrol car. Another held his side where Steve had slammed into him.

Steroids weren't for nothing, were they, loser?

Too numb to process what had happened, Benson mumbled, "Is Colin going to die?"

"I, um, I don't know, son…" Mr. Traynor's eyes filled with tears, and Benson suddenly separated.

No longer there, he felt outside himself, a familiar surge of anger welling deep inside him. Sizzling next to it was an overwhelming sadness. He watched someone photographing Steve and the blood trail that streaked the concrete and splattered surrounding cars. Ralston's motionless body held no satisfaction. Nothing felt vindicated.

He just felt alone. Scores of people now surrounded the parking garage trying to get a better look at what had happened. The area crawled with officers, medics, and suited men with serious expressions. None of it made sense.

That reporter looks familiar…why am I here? Benson couldn't remember…

"Oh, crap," Ryan muttered and scrambled for something white that had slid underneath the car.

The letter! The memory slithered back, and fragments scrambled about in Benson's brain. He stared at Mr. Ralston, who crouched next to Steve, "Check again! He can't be dead! NO!"

Turning back to Ryan, Benson opened his mouth to speak. Nothing came out. Mr. Traynor locked eyes with him, but everything swam out of focus.

He didn't feel a thing on his way down.

Benson's Journal

Wednesday, September 24th
   Mom and Dad are at the hospital with Colin. He's in ICU. He's not awake. He's on life support.

Thursday, September 25th
   Mom and Dad are at the hospital with Colin. He's in ICU. He still hasn't woken up. He's still on life support.

Friday, September 26th
   Friends keep calling, I keep having to repeat myself, and it's weird that I can't say much without a blob clogging my throat. Even when I see Colin, I want to touch him, to say something, to make him wake up, but I can't talk. What would I say? And I'm pissed that Steve Ralston died. I wanted to kill him myself. At least my broken fingers, hand cast and all, can vouch for my payback. Asshole.

Saturday, September 27th
   I'm at the hospital with Mom and Dad. Colin's still in ICU, but his vitals, Dr. Hough said, aren't good. He probably won't make it through the night…Me either.
Monday, September 29th
   The funeral is Wednesday.

Ryan's Journal

Saturday, September 27th

Mrs. Matt, if you're out there, I really need your help. Benson's on the verge of a serious breakdown, and I don't know what to do. I've called, I've gone to see him, but he's like a robot. He barely talks, he repeats the same phrases over and over, and I think Colin isn't going to make it. If Colin dies, I'm not sure what'll happen to my best friend. What do I do, Mrs. Matt? How do I help?

Sunday, September 28th

Spent the day at the hospital with Benson and his family. Colin died at 3:21 p.m., which is weird...that's his birthday...March 21st, I mean.

Benson handled it better than his parents, but he still barely talks. Hope he gets back to his old self eventually, but I won't rush him. I can't imagine what he's feeling. I just want to help. I told him Colin would be with you now, Mrs. Matt, and that seemed to help a little. Maybe that was your plan all along. Who knows?

Lots of funerals this week, but I don't think I'll go to any except yours and Colin's. Tim's out of the hospital, so maybe he can come too.

Benson isn't coming to school for a week or two. I don't blame him. Who can think about homework right now? Classes start back Tuesday, but from what I hear, tons of kids have transferred or aren't coming back until after all the funerals. I know there's one almost every day this week, but yours is tomorrow. That's why we're out of school.

Chapter 22

AT MRS. MATTINGLY'S funeral, little could be heard except crying. And no matter how much Pam, Tim, and several other people tried, Benson spoke to no one but Ryan. Words wouldn't matter, not anymore.

People asked about the punch, the parking garage, but Benson couldn't talk about it yet. He could barely talk at all. Many signed his cast, and he would stare at the things they wrote.

You Rock!

Punch of the decade

The shot that will ring in infamy

He fingered the cast and wondered what had possessed him to hit Steve. He'd never had the courage or desire to do anything like that before.

He took a seat in a pew next to Ryan. Someone asked him a question, but that crazy blob filled his throat again. His parents hadn't attended Mrs. Matt's funeral with him. They had barely gotten out of bed since coming home from the hospital Sunday evening. His mom had said little, and what few words had come out of his dad's mouth made no sense.

They both drank a lot, barely ate, and seemed to have forgotten Colin wasn't their only son.

Ryan's parents let Benson stay at their house Monday and Tuesday, and he couldn't thank them enough for that. His house felt like a strange museum. Colin's bedroom door hadn't been opened, and he knew everything behind it was exactly as he'd left it the last time he had snooped.

Shame shoved the lump deeper, almost gagging him. For a second, he worried he was going to be sick.

"Ben?" Ryan's face blurred in front of him. All Benson could do was shake his head.

He'd called his parents, told them he was going to Mrs. Matt's funeral that afternoon. All his mom could say was how much she loved him. When she couldn't stop crying, he told her he'd be home that evening and hung up. Mrs. Laughlin thought it best that he be back home with his family. He begged Ryan to spend the night, but she said, "Not this time, Benson. Your parents need you now."

What about me? he wanted to say but didn't.

The blob probably would've prevented it anyhow.

When Mr. Mattingly stood and walked to the podium, the bawling became almost unbearable. Benson made no effort to wipe away the tears streaming down his cheeks. Somehow it felt good to wallow, to let the sorrow consume him. If he thought about anything too hard, the police parking garage swam back into focus, and all he could smell was gunpowder and blood.

It had more than replaced the Media Center.

Sitting in the church, he stared forward unseeing, wishing he could back up time. He wouldn't even mind Colin plowing him over the ottoman in the living room or hogging the remote. The lump swelled in his throat again until he thought he would suffocate. He'd cried so much, he couldn't breathe through his nose anymore. Ryan shuddered. Benson took a quick glance...his best friend's eyes were as red as the velvet seats, and a tear dripped from the tip of Ryan's nose onto trembling hands. Benson dropped his gaze before Ryan caught him staring.

It's not just me...

The revelation walloped him, sucked the last of his air, and flip-flopped the self-pity in his gut. Colin wasn't the only one who'd died.

The epiphany didn't make it go away. Tears only fell faster now.

As they shuffled out of the church, Ryan pulled a Kleenex from his pocket and blew his nose. "I can't go back to her class," he blurted.

"We have to," Benson answered, and he suddenly got it. No lights went on over his head, but it was just as obvious. "Ryan, it's what she'd want. Operation Cappuccino is pretty much finished. We don't need the interviews, because what happened answered our questions, didn't it?" Benson stopped and stared at everyone streaming out of the church. Red faces, bloodshot eyes, and a symphony of sniffles. He held his cast, thinking for the first time what a pain not having his right hand would be at school, but there were more important things now, weren't there? He was glad he had a few weeks off. His parents were leaving it up to him when he would go back.

Maybe never... But he knew that wasn't true. Drowning himself in self-pity could only go on so long until he'd need to come up for air.

Ryan turned to him. "God, you're right." He sighed, and when Mr. and Mrs. Laughlin emerged with numerous sets of parents, the boys fell in behind them and trudged silently to the car.

When the Laughlins dropped him off in his driveway, he told Ryan to call him after school the next day to fill him in on all the details.

Ryan laughed. "I'm not calling you, you moron. I'll be over at 3:30. Be up and showered by then, okay?"

Benson managed a smile and headed toward his house. There seemed to be a dark cloud hovering over it. Flowers were wilting from lack of rain and impending autumn, a broken wheelbarrow leaned beside the garage door, and the lawn needed raking in the worst way. He didn't want to go inside, so he plopped down on the front steps. When a wrecker pulled in front of the house with Colin's Mazda in tow, Benson wondered when the triggers were ever going to stop. He raced inside and up the stairs to bawl in peace.

* * *

"Benson?" his mom called through his door sometime later. Her voice sounded almost normal, pre-Black Monday, pre-parking garage.

I'm an only child now.

A wave of sorrow made him gag until he spit up in his trashcan. His mom barged into his room.

"Benson, are you okay, honey?" She sat beside him and rubbed his back. Then a strange connection jolted through him as he turned to her. Even though her eyes were swollen and she looked ten years older, the glimmer of Momhood had returned to them.

"Mom, I...I need to tell you some things." Benson bowed his head, and all the activities of the previous week spilled out – Operation Cappuccino, getting close to Colin, and the guilt he felt about instigating Steve Ralston. For some weird reason, he even shared about the time in fourth grade when they played their cruel game of Red Rover with him. He left out details about the letter jacket and the condoms. Some secrets had to be kept, for Colin's sake.

When he finished, his mother held him. After a few minutes, she whispered, "I love you so much, Benson, and nothing you did or didn't do could've caused or changed anything." She sniffled, then leaned back, brushed the hair from his eyes, and stared hard into them. "Do you hear me? Steve Ralston had this in him long before your interview. Long before." She sighed and plopped her hands on her blue-jeaned thighs. He liked his mom's quiet strength and was grateful she was regaining it. Seeing both his parents broken had scared him worse than the Media Center and parking garage combined.

"D...do you think Colin saw me hit Steve?" That blob leapt into Benson's throat, and with concerted effort, he kept it from choking him.

His mom smiled through fresh tears, and for a fraction of a second, he thought she was going to laugh. "Yes, he saw it, and I bet he would high-five you for it." Tears streamed down her face, but she continued to smile.

When she left his room, Benson thought about that for a long time – Colin high-fiving him for popping Ralston in the mouth. It had hurt something fierce, and just thinking about it made his hand throb. He read some of the inscriptions again and wondered how that punch would change him or his place on the social food chain.

He should've had a clue, but in the wake of losing his

brother, Benson hadn't thought about it.

What surprised him most was that he really didn't care.

Chapter 23

HIS FIRST DAY back to school – almost two weeks after Colin's funeral – couldn't have been harder for Benson. Aside from avoiding all the places that had been repainted, everyone hovered over him, asking him to replay the whole police station incident and how it felt to be famous. People were too consumed with the punch to consider that his brother had died that day. The ever-present blob wedged permanently in his throat the entire day. When the final bell rang, Benson decided it had been such a bizarre day, it might've been a dream.

Students he'd never met followed him, kids who had turned their noses up before the punch now hung on every word he said, and the Barbie Brigade somehow forgot that he had recently dwelled in geekdom.

"You're coming to Primrose after school, aren't you, Benson?" Mallorie wandered past him toward Cheerleader Corner. She had called him several times over the course of the past weeks, though they had only talked about superficial things.

"Yeah, don't be late!" Jenni Waterman added as Nikki Harmon clanked her locker shut.

"I want to sign your cast, Benson, so hurry up!" Nikki grabbed Jenni by the arm and waltzed away.

"Is that for real?" Benson asked Ryan. He realized his mouth was hanging open and clamped it shut. They tossed their books into the locker and grabbed their backpacks.

"Holy crap," Ryan muttered, and after a few minutes of debating, the boys decided they should go.

"I want to, but let's keep it business-like...for our project." Benson added. "I mean, I don't wanna hang with them...do you?"

"No way. But we can't turn back now. What'll it hurt?"

Ryan shrugged his shoulders.

"True." Benson nodded, and the two set off down the hall. Neither said anything else as they set out for *the* hangout for everyone who mattered.

They hustled to the diner, the day swirling in Benson's head. Teachers had welcomed him back, and each gave him a pat on his left hand or a squeeze as if to say, *We're here for you.*

The anger was gone. A strange *I'm okay* had replaced it.

In Publications, the new teacher had said they would reassess the direction of the class, but the boys agreed they would finish Operation Cappuccino anyway. No one talked much, but during the days he'd been gone, she had taken it upon herself to devise a weekly newspaper that would include interviews with Westwood's most prominent alumni. Benson had wanted to gag. *Mrs. Matt would want to recognize ALL alumni, not just the popular ones.* But he smiled and took his assignment without even reading it.

There was a new P.E. teacher filling in until Coach Rohart came back, and a permanent substitute had taken over for Ms. Waters. Students said they heard she was taking a leave of absence. The rumor was that she wasn't coming back at all.

Benson had a fleeting image of Ms. Waters crouched inside the Media Center doors as Mrs. Matt dashed into the hallway. Bile rose in his throat as he and Ryan reached the crosswalk near the diner.

"I can't believe we're actually going." Benson waited for the guard to usher them across the street. Six or seven grade schoolers from nearby Field milled around them.

"We don't have to stay long." Ryan switched his backpack to his other shoulder, then added, "I'm hungry anyway, aren't you?"

The light changed, and they headed toward the brightly decorated diner, designed to look like an old 1950s hangout.

"No." Benson heaved a sigh. Food didn't have much appeal to him these days. They paused outside the door before he finally yanked it open.

"Hi, Benson," Mallorie called out, patting the seat next to

her in the semi-circle corner booth. "How's your hand? Can I sign it?"

He'd wondered why she hadn't asked yet. But then he'd only spoken to her a couple of times since the hospital. His first day back, she hadn't swooped in like the rest of the vultures.

Another girl sat Ryan down on the opposite corner. The booth was meant for five, but eight kids were crammed around the table. All of them suddenly took great pains to sign Benson's cast before he had a chance to even say anything. Some of them already had, but what was he supposed to say? *One signature limit?*

He wondered who several of the unfamiliar faces were. No one bothered with introductions, and some of them signed his cast with curly-cues and elaborately designed initials.

They just assume everyone knows who they are.

"I'm so sorry about Colin." Mallorie paused. Her lip quivered a little. "Allison and I both thought he was really nice." She glanced at the girl sitting by Ryan.

Several other kids offered condolences, but Benson held up his hand. "Thanks, but... I can't talk about it." His gut churned and images of the parking garage flashed in his head. The lump gelled and quadrupled in size while the familiar sting of gunpowder burned his nostrils. Tears threatened to send him scurrying for the bathroom.

Ryan tried to small talk with the girl next to him – Allison – and Benson wanted to thank his best friend for the diversion. The others began to share what the first week back had been like and then how the following week had almost been normal.

The daily gathering, Nikki said, was like a tribute to Megan. All her friends drinking sodas, talking, remembering. They even tried to laugh at what she would think of it all, but Mallorie sniffled, and it was all Benson could do to keep his own tears in check. He watched her stare at the table, picking at a chip in the Formica. He wanted to say something, but he couldn't think of anything important enough to say out loud in front of everyone.

Nikki, sitting next to Allison, reached across the table and squeezed Mallorie's left hand. The gesture tugged at Benson's heart. Mallorie suddenly dropped her right hand onto the seat between them and laced her fingers into his left hand.

Just like that, he was holding her hand. Or rather, *she* was holding *his* hand. It sent a zip through his insides.

Much to his relief, Ryan grinned. Benson couldn't decide if he liked her being straightforward or resented the assumption that he liked her.

But he *did* like her, didn't he? Maybe that was her way of asking for comfort, and offering it. Strangely, it made him feel better. Almost safe.

"Did you read the letter Colin gave you? Everybody's wondering. It's like our last piece of Megan," Allison said, not thinking how it might make him feel.

Ahhhh. Explains the invite.

Benson knew he shouldn't have shown the letter off at the hospital the way he had. But now that they knew, they felt entitled. It made him nauseous to sit there and pretend he could be one of them.

"How did you hear about the letter?" he asked bluntly. Allison hadn't been one of the girls at the hospital, not that he could remember anyway. He liked that he was becoming stronger, not because of the spotlight but in spite of it. He didn't want to appear insensitive, but he also wasn't going to be manipulated. Having been in spotlight all day, like he was Brad Pitt, had altered his perception of all of them.

"Word gets around," Nikki said, and fingered the Blue Jays' ribbon around her wrist. "Last week Lisa talked with Sherrie who was sleeping over at Stephanie's. And her dorky little brother is a good friend of Tim Silvey's. Apparently, Tim knew all about it, even shared how Ryan had rescued one of the copies in the parking garage. It's all pretty scary, isn't it? And your famous punch, Benson. You're all the talk at school."

Benson glared at Ryan, who suddenly found great interest in more loose Formica at the edge of the table. But he couldn't blame Ryan, because they all wanted to be part of something, didn't they?

"What about the letter, Benson? Do you have it? We heard

you're the only person other than the police who has a copy. That's what your brother gave you in the hospital while we were there, isn't it?" Nikki Harmon stared at him again, obviously still skeptical of his inclusion in their group, even if he *was* all the talk.

Benson reciprocated any feelings for her that she had for him. He didn't trust her or like her. Something about Nikki seemed plastic. And he wanted to tell her she had no right to talk about his brother, indirectly connected or not.

"I don't have the letter with me. And even if I did, I wouldn't let you read it. Any of you." He refrained from mentioning he hadn't read the famous letter himself. He and Ryan had discussed it, but he hadn't been able to actually do it yet. He wondered fleetingly if his parents had read Detective McElhaney's copy.

"That letter could answer a lot of questions, Benson, ease people's minds. You don't realize how hard the *not knowing* is. They don't say anything that matters on the news, and now that there won't be a trial...I just can't imagine what came over Steve to do something so...so...*extreme*." Jenni Waterman shook her head as she sipped her soda.

"Mallorie, you were Megan's best friend, and even you don't know why all this happened. What if things in that letter could help us all, Benson, especially Mallorie?" Nikki glared at him now, her eyes smoldering, and he thought any minute Superman-like lasers would burn a hole through him.

Everyone sat silent.

"Sorry," he muttered, but the only thing he was sorry for was not having the guts to get up and walk out.

"Hey, that reporter's gonna write the book," Ryan offered.

Benson fought the urge to grin, but Mallorie let out a sigh, then pulled her hand from his. The message seemed clear. Fork over the famous letter, and the dreg days would be over. In large part, their status had changed with the swing of that famous punch anyway.

But now, Benson knew withholding the letter could reverse that. If he didn't give it up, he could be resigned to being social sediment forever.

"What are you afraid of, Benson?" a mousy dark-headed girl sitting next to Nikki asked. Her eyes scrunched close enough together to touch, and Benson thought it made her look more like a rat than a mouse. She wasn't a cheerleader but had status anyway, either via money or address, he didn't know. She didn't need letters, punches, or big brothers.

He heard Colin's voice in his head as clear as if he'd had earphones on. *Don't be a spectator, Bennie...it's not about being me anymore.*

He heaved a sigh, really thinking about what he felt. "Betrayal. Something all of you are very good at. I understand what you're feeling, ladies. It's an emotion Ryan and I live with every day. But I made a promise to my brother that I intend to keep." He held his breath, waiting for their comebacks. He didn't know if he had to keep that promise anymore, but he sure didn't intend to share his brother's insight with the Barbie Brigade.

"It's okay, Benson. Actually, that's really sweet," Mallorie finally said. She patted the back of his hand. The gesture made him feel better, almost as if she were defying the group. But she didn't take his hand again.

Allison nodded and dropped her eyes before anyone could say anything.

"Don't lie to him, Mallorie," Rat Girl said. "You didn't sleep last night. You haven't slept in days. Don't be selfish and insensitive, Benson. Even Ryan said he wanted to read the letter. It's not like Colin will know."

Benson's mouth fell open. *You got some nerve... who the hell are you anyway?*

Ryan found interest in a chipped section of the table again, but Benson didn't care. That wasn't what had his blood boiling.

"I don't even know you," he blurted. "And you're judging me? What would you do if Megan had left you a letter and begged you not to read it or let anyone else read it? Would you screw that loyalty just to please a bunch of...of...friends?"

No one said a word. *Friends* hadn't been the word dancing on the tip of his tongue.

It would've pissed them off, and they wouldn't have

skipped a beat before telling me to get lost. At least this way, they have to at least acknowledge how selfish they are. Maybe...

The silence and lowered eyes lasted longer than Benson expected. He turned to Mallorie, whose bowed head made it impossible to read her expression. "What would you do, Mallorie?"

She looked up, and he flinched at the tear that slid down her cheek. "I'd do what you're doing. Or...or God, I don't know, because it's *not* me. But it is hard, Benson. You get to know what we don't."

"I *get* to know?" Benson's voice was louder than he meant for it to be. He felt their stares, like a lab rat waiting to be torn apart. He envisioned Nikki with a scalpel hovering over his brain and, in a maniacal voice squealing for everyone to stand back, she was going in.

He smiled in spite of the situation or the ache in his heart. *Colin would be proud...* Thinking about his brother catapulted the blob halfway up his throat.

"Well, now that's a wicked grin, Benson." Mallorie's eyes narrowed, but she gave a hint of a smile. She was watching him closely. He refused to notice her, *really* notice her. As sad as they might be, none of them had watched their own brother shot and killed.

The mental admission almost squeezed his throat closed.

"Sorry," he mumbled again, but the old surge of anger reared its ugly head inside him. Something about the past weeks had hardened him to their conceit. Sarcasm lingered just behind his pursed lips, and it took a lot of effort to keep his mouth shut.

The attention didn't make him feel as slimy as he thought it would. *This wouldn't be so bad...for the right reasons.*

But this wasn't it. The Barbie Brigade oozed superiority, and it made him want to puke.

Were they a product of nature or nurture? He couldn't imagine how he had grown up in the same environment but had turned out so differently. Even Colin never disregarded people the way the Barbies did. Not even when he picked on Benson.

You're all clones. He envisioned rows of robot warriors in *Star Wars* coming to life. The image brought another faint smile to his face.

"Penny for your thoughts," Mallorie probed again.

"Just thinking about the irony of all this."

Why lie?

"All what?"

Can you really be that clueless, Mallorie?

"Oh, a few weeks ago you thought I was Colin Schmidt's geeky younger brother, wondering how I could *not worry* what anyone thought of me. And that made me strange. Remember? At the lockers?" Benson's heart raced. Heat crept up his neck and into his face. He couldn't believe he had said it, but he felt wildly free at having the guts.

Yeah, Colin would be proud...

"Ah, c'mon, we don't think that," she started, but Benson quickly interrupted her.

"Don't patronize me, Mallorie," he said, repeating his mother's favorite expression. "I heard everything you all said about me that Friday before the shooting. When I was at my locker, and you were all talking about Michael and Steve? The conversation makes me sick now that I know about Megan and my brother. She couldn't even own up to how she felt about him months after they started going out. And you knew. The others may not've, but *you* did."

There. I said it.

The hateful voice in his head itched for a podium. Why couldn't he control that monster? At least the throat blob had diminished enough to let the words pass.

Mallorie hung her head in shame. She said nothing. What could she say? It frustrated Benson that she didn't come clean.

"You knew, Mallorie?" Nikki stopped playing with her wrist ribbon to stare at her friend.

"Is that true, Mall?" Allison asked.

But Mallorie sat silent, not moving or looking at any of them.

"I thought so." Benson stood and motioned to Ryan. "We'll see you around."

He hadn't meant to create all this drama...that was more Brigade style. And he knew once he walked out the door, he might be a dreg forever. But being a dreg felt different now. It didn't feel forced on him. They had bridged the gap but he was okay with hanging with the lower half. He'd seen firsthand that the social structure was weakest at the top.

I wanna be like Colin...to earn my way there by being friends with people I choose.

"Wait, Benson. Don't go," one of them called out.

He about-faced and nearly ran into Ryan.

Nikki Harmon waited for his full attention.

"Sit back down, please." She motioned toward the seat he'd just left.

He hesitated. Ryan raised his eyebrows, staring at Benson.

"No thanks, Nikki. I'm sipping cappuccinos with snobs when I'm really just a soda kinda guy. See ya around."

His exit proved more dramatic than he intended. He felt the eyes bore into his back and didn't turn to see if his best friend was following. He did, however, hear Nikki mutter something to her worshippers about losers and missed opportunities.

He was stunned when Ryan snapped, "Screw you, Nikki. You haven't had an original thought since you dyed your hair last year. You and Ralston are cut from the same cloth, and it ain't silk."

For the first time in his near-adult life, Benson Michael Schmidt understood that opportunities came and they went.

It was what you did in between that counted.

Colin's Letter

TO MEGAN'S FAMILY, the police, and my parents,

I'm writing this letter to aid in the conviction of Steve Ralston. Whatever comes of this situation, he had a history of violence well before Monday's shooting at Westwood, and I really want to set some things straight.

Last May, Steve Ralston started using steroids to buff up so he could make the varsity team. He told me and several other guys, and he knew we wouldn't tell because quite a few of them are juicing, too. But then Steve moved on to cocaine to "smooth out the edges," he said. Before that, he smoked marijuana and took speed, but nothing that really affected his personality the way the coke and steroids did.

His ex-girlfriend, Megan Barker, tried to stop him. He not only didn't listen, he tried to shut her up. Twice. Each incident occurred on Friday nights after an evening of drinking, snorting, and partying with friends.

He sexually assaulted Megan both times and told her he'd do it again if she ever spoke another word about his drug use. Or of what he'd done to her. So she only told her best friend and made her swear not to tell. He said he would do the same thing to anybody and everybody she told.

That's when she confided in me.

We met at a mixer after a Friday night rave in June. She knew who I was because of sports. I knew who she was because of her brother.

We hit it off and started talking on the phone, going out to private places. That's when she told me about Steve. The drugs and the rapes. She was humiliated and thought it was her fault. She didn't feel she could tell anyone or get help because he'd flip out.

She was right.

The shooting Monday was partly my fault because Megan had on my letter jacket. That set Steve off. But it was all blowing up before that.

What Megan said to him that day was why he went home to get his dad's gun. I'm certain he shot her for something she said, and the worst part is...it was a lie.

Megan called me Sunday night and said she was going to tell Steve she was pregnant – with my baby. She hoped that would send him away once and for all. She said he would realize how serious we were, and she was going to tell him I had truly been her first since the only two times they'd been together had been assaults.

She never dreamed he would snap the way he did. I know the drugs, especially the juice, didn't help. I also know the baby wasn't mine. She and I had gone to a clinic about her getting an abortion, because it was Steve's from when he raped her. I didn't deny it to Mr. Barker because I wanted them to find out the right way. I wasn't going to sit and deny it like some stupid kid. Not until I could prove it.

I was strong in my convictions because Megan and I never slept together, not that we didn't want to, but we never did. She couldn't, and I respected her too much to push. The thought of it freaked her out after what Steve had done to her. She only told Steve the baby was mine to get him to leave her alone.

So the baby he killed was his own. The saddest part is, he never considered that the baby could actually be his. He just saw it for how it affected his precious reputation.

My little brother told me something that really made me think. He called himself a dreg. Said he didn't blend in with the cliques like I did, that the popular people are the mixers, and others settle to the bottom to be nobodies.

Thing is, I have always felt a little like a dreg. I don't like the mixing, the attention, and the hype. I only like being out on the court or the field so I can lose myself in the feel of the moment. It isn't about winning or being the best, but the rush of competing. I never needed the juice...the game was my juice.

I hope when all this is over, Steve gets his, and everybody else sees that being popular isn't "all that."

The attention isn't all it's cracked up to be.

It's sure changed my perspective on life. At least now I get the important things, like friends and family.

Life's too short to mess with the petty stuff.

Colin Schmidt

Chapter 24

BENSON BLINKED BACK tears as he read his brother's name out loud and smoothed the crinkled letter. Ryan wiped his own eyes, but played like it was no biggie.

But it was. They agreed Colin would've been okay with them reading the letter now, and Ryan suggested Benson read it out loud. By the end, the lump had shoved its way into the base of his throat, making it tough to continue.

Neither of them spoke when he finished. What could they say? The ticking clock and hum of the muted TV accompanied Benson's chaotic thoughts. All the recent attention over the punch, telling the Barbie Brigade they weren't all that, and realizing he and Ryan might not be dregs anymore. They assumed one or all of the Barbies must've written the anonymous note and Benson still didn't know what was in it. *Would the police ever figure it out?*

He figured it didn't matter now. And like it or not, the world had shifted.

We might not like the heat of the spotlight, but we're on the sidelines doing our own thing, and we're part of things in our own way.

Benson liked the idea, liked the prospect of spectating or playing, depending on his mood. He wouldn't let the crowd dictate to him anymore. From now on, he would seize Colin's mentality.

Life's too short to mess with the petty stuff.

Chapter 25
September, the next school year

"HEY, BONEHEAD, DON'T eat my burger!" A kid punched a boy sitting next to him.

Benson did a double-take as he walked into the cafeteria and realized the arguing boys were twins.

"Don't let him snort milk or I swear to God, I'm gonna puke," Tim ordered from another area of the lunchroom. "Hey, Benson, tell 'em!"

Benson grinned. Scooter was at it again, because it always got a laugh, no matter how much Tim hated it.

Walking into the cafeteria on his first day as an eighth grader seemed different. He wasn't low man on the totem pole anymore. Not quite the power of a freshman, but certainly with a little of the middleman clout. And no longer just a spectator. He owed that to Colin.

"Yo, Schmitty, come sit down!" Someone motioned to a seat at the table nearest the check-out line. A few other soccer players milled around it in their own jerseys. He had worn his just like they'd agreed.

He gave them an *in a minute* sign as he searched the cafeteria.

"Hey, Bennie! Over here! How was Algebra? You looked a little panicky heading to class!"

"Oh, bite me, Ryan," he snipped, but laughed as he headed toward his best friend. "Not everybody's brain is a calculator. Just wait 'til you have Honors English. You'll be knocking down my door. How was advanced math, anyway?"

"Easy, man, piece of cake." Ryan rolled his eyes.

The two bantered, hit fists, and Benson joined them in the middle of the cafeteria. Peace stickers were already plastered on a variety of the tables, much to the chagrin of the janitors and cooks who had to remove them. But in the grand scheme of problems, it rated low for most of the Westwood administration. It even proved a bit of an omen for a better school year.

Both boys studied the seating around them. Football players wandered from table to table. A few cheerleader types grouped near the front, but they mingled throughout the lunchroom.

Benson smiled. It seemed like the whole Steve thing might finally become part of the school's history and not the day-to-day obsession it had been. The sensationalized gun battle. The funerals and emotional recovery of the student body. The media frenzy over Megan's pregnancy. Once the DNA results verified paternity, Benson and his parents had agreed to an interview with the Jamestown Daily News and had shared some of the letter with them to "set the record straight," his dad claimed. They *didn't* grant interviews to the jerk reporter writing the book. Benson thought that would make Mrs. Matt proud.

He had even been in the paper himself. In the spring, he and Ryan shared details about *Operation Cappuccino* and how frustrated they'd been with the power of popularity. The school newspaper ran the article after it appeared in the Jamestown Daily News.

And then everything at school started changing. Subtly, at first, but everyone understood the impact of what had happened at Westwood and in Jamestown. And the infamous punch helped his credibility.

"Okay, boys. Are you gonna let a few girls make this table politically correct?"

They looked up at Mallorie Taylor and Nikki Harmon standing in their rah-rah skirts. Allison Peters – the cheerleader Ryan voted Most Likely to Be Featured in the Sports Illustrated Swimsuit Issue – be-bopped up behind her fellow Brigaders.

"Hmmm, I don't know, Benson, whaddya think?" Ryan cocked his head, rubbed his chin, and pretended to ponder their proposal.

"Only if they come bearing gifts," Benson teased, grabbing the Pepsi from Mallorie's tray. He popped it open and took a huge swallow.

She sat down and smacked him on the arm. "Don't drink it all, Benson. You're such a mooch."

"I know," he answered. "I got it from my brother."

Everyone fell silent for a brief moment. Benson let the wave of remembering pass through him, a long ago time when he and Colin got excused from the dinner table for the belching game his mother insisted they needed to outgrow – quickly. He cocked an eyebrow, swallowed several gulps of air, then ripped his best burp yet.

"You're so gross, Benson. Just when I think you might walk upright, those knuckles scrape the ground." Nikki curled a disgusted lip.

Benson wanted to tell her the sneer made her look like Elvis.

"That is gross, Benson, for real," Allison said, and dropped onto the seat next to Ryan.

"I give it an 8.7," Ryan countered.

"8.7, my butt. That was a 9.5, at least!" Benson frowned and tossed his napkin to signify his distaste with the score. He darted his eyes to see if Mallorie had smiled. She had.

"You guys really are losers." Nikki got up and stormed toward the table filled with other skirts. A black-and-white composition book slipped out from under her binder and clattered to the table. Benson snatched it.

He read the cover, *The Diva Diary.* He thumbed through it and exclaimed, "Hey, are these my initials?" Turning the last few pages, he glared from Nikki to Allison to Mallorie.

"Give me that, Benson Schmidt, right now!" Nikki tried to grab the notebook, but he stood and held it too high for her. "That's MINE!"

With one hand, he kept her back and read, *"Skye, I know you like BS, so spill the dirt. Give up the details. Lady Di.* Who the heck is that?"

Mallorie turned bright red but said nothing.

"BENSON!" Nikki shouted.

Benson squinted, analyzing her, and gave a smug nod. "Ah, that's *gotta* be you." He read on. *"Yes, Di, but Jade likes RL too, so don't get all bent over it."* He looked at Mallorie. "Who's Jade?"

"We have code names – our birthstones. That's enough, Benson, please. Give it back."

He grinned but relinquished the composition book to Nikki. "I'm not calling you Lady Di...besides, that's not a birthstone."

"Diamond, you moron, for April. I just shortened it." Nikki huffed off with the notebook, ranting to someone that she would be glad when she got to high school and didn't have to deal with children and Neanderthals.

"Of course she would shorten it to make herself a princess," Ryan scoffed.

"Guess things haven't changed as much as we thought." Benson shrugged. "So you must be *Skye*? What's *that* short for?"

"Long story," Mallorie mumbled. "You're definitely a work in progress."

Allison nodded, but a smile pushed at the edges of her mouth.

"I'm open for construction," Ryan insisted, and sat up tall in case they hadn't noticed he'd grown three inches over the summer. "Interested in the position...*Jade?*"

Allison gave a mocking scowl then handed him a napkin. "You have mustard on your mouth."

Ryan laughed, making himself choke, nearly losing the half-chewed bite of sandwich in the process. Benson burped and gave an exaggerated smear of his hand across his nose and mouth.

The sarcasm evaporated as he caught a glimpse of the new motto painted bright blue along the side wall of the cafeteria. The foot-high words pierced through him. Things *had* changed. The motto was the same one now displayed in the gym, the media center, and on banners in the hallway. After the school had been repainted, the student council came up with the saying and voted to adopt it during the spring election. When they returned from Easter break, students had been amazed to see it on every major hallway of Westwood Junior High. And Benson embraced the words with every moment he lived. For Mrs. Matt and especially for Colin.

Mallorie saw him staring at the sign and squeezed his hand.

Blue Jays don't have status. They all fly with the same wings.

Colin had known it, and Benson wished he had figured it out sooner. Whether he sipped lattes with the Brigade or burped when he swigged a soda, he now understood that the only difference between a rut and a grave was who did the measuring.

He'd use his own yardstick from now on.

The End

Author Biography

Barri L. Bumgarner was not a dreg, though by college, she had a pretty nasty case of geek-envy. It wasn't until she was a junior high teacher that she saw the true and harsh realities of today's cliques. It became her mission to show teenagers that after high school, no one cares what brand of jeans you wore or who you dated. Bill Gates is proof of that.

After high school, Barri expanded her ring of friends to include dregs, dweebs, geeks, and posers – you know who you are.

She currently lives in Columbia, Missouri with her two fox terriers, both of whom have many friends from various cliques. Lilah is even considering marrying Farley, a preppy cocker spaniel.

To keep tabs on potential dates for the ceremony, visit: www.barrilbumgarner.com. You can even also keep up on her life as an author.

Kaycey, left, and Lilah

Printed in the United States
79391LV00004B/4-6